The Invasion of Planet Wampetter

The Invasion of Planet Wampetter

Samuel H. Pillsbury

Illustrated by Matthew Angorn

Perspective Publishing

Los Angeles

Library of Congress Catalog Card Number
ISBN 0-9622036-6-1

Published by
Perspective Publishing, Inc., 50 S. DeLacey Ave. Suite 201
Pasadena, CA 91105, (818)440-9635

Additional copies of this book may be ordered by calling toll free 1-800-992-6657, or by sending $18.50 ($15 + $3.50 shipping) to above address. CA residents add sales tax. Discounts available for quantity orders.

Library of Congress Cataloging-in-Publication Data

Pillsbury, Samuel H.
The invasion of planet Wampetter / Samuel H. Pillsbury ; illustrated by Matthew Angorn.
p cm.
Summary: The Tub family saves their planet from being destroyed by intergalactic tourism while recognizing that they have much to offer and to learn from visitors.
ISBN 0-9622036-6-1
[1. Science fiction.] I. Angorn, Matthew, 1971- ill.
II. Title.
PZ7 . P6316In 1995
[Fic] -- dc20 95-8432
CIP
AC

Printed in Canada
First Edition

For Leah and Allison

Contents

CHAPTER ONE

The Arrival

Planet Wampetter has always been an easy place to visit. It's not that far, really, just the other side of the galaxy. You don't need a special application or photographs or shots. If you want to go to Planet Wampetter, you just fuel up your ship, set the computer and off you go. That's the way it is. That's the way it's always been.

Still, Planet Wampetter has not been a popular travel destination. In fact, creatures all over the galaxy love to tell mean jokes about the place. For example, "How many seasons are there on Planet Wampetter?" Answer: "Two. Too hot and too cold." Or, "Where did the stupidhead go to for vacation?" Answer: "Planet Wampetter. Why do you think he's called a stupid-head?" Yet there was a time not so very long ago when large numbers of galactic visitors descended on Planet Wampetter. For a while it appeared the planet might become the hot new tourist destination. In fact for a while it *was* the hot new tourist destination. This is the story of how that happened and what happened next.

Eloise Tub and her sister Gartrude were playing brontosaurus in the mud patch behind their house. This traditional wampetter game involves stomping slowly in the mud and making awful braying sounds like this: AAUUUUNNNNEEEEEEIII!! It was Change Season, the rainy period between winter and summer. Eloise and Gartrude were covered with mud, which turned their clothes and orange skins a deep reddish brown. They were handsome wampetter children: plump and energetic, with big noses, bigger voices and eyes as bright as the sun glinting off Lake Wacawacawoo in the morning.

Suddenly a small space ship dropped out of the sky into the field across the street. It was a kind they had seen only on the bigscreen; they knew it was very expensive. Out of the ship came a family of humans, looking rather purplish in the planet's red light, and to wampetter eyes, particularly slim, graceful and sophisticated. There was a mother, a father, and three boys; each carried a small shiny metal suitcase. After much pointing and discussion, the humans set down their suitcases, opened them and stepped back. Gartrude and Eloise gaped in wonder.

"Eloise, look, it's growing!" Gartrude said, pointing.

"Don't point, it's rude. Besides, it's not growing, it's—it's—expanding."

Each of the suitcases expanded into a room and then linked together to form hallways and a whole

first floor, then a second and a third, followed by a rooftop turret and large windows, indeed all the accoutrements of a fancy house, the likes of which the wampetter girls had never seen—except on the bigscreen.

"Let's go over and say hi," Gartrude suggested.

"But we're all dirty," Eloise objected.

"That's perfect!" Gartrude said. Indeed on Planet Wampetter, visitors often take a mud bath before going visiting. Having your face caked with mud and bits of food from your last meal is the height of wampetter fashion. Eloise knew that wampetter customs varied a bit from those of other creatures, though, and she did not want to say anything to these new visitors until she had consulted her handy *How Not to Insult An Alien and Get Your Head Chopped Off, a handbook for travelling wampetters,* which they had at home. But Gartrude just ran over to the humans and Eloise had to follow.

"I'm Gartrude, this is my sister Eloise. We're wampetters and you're not!" Gartrude announced.

Eloise was appalled, but the humans seemed amused by the small rotund creature with the eager smile. Fortunately Gartrude had not used any of the more traditional wampetter greetings like "You look like you're about to barf," or "You look so fat you could explode."

Eloise was terribly impressed with the family up close. The father was tall and handsome, and the mother was simply the most beautiful creature Eloise had ever encountered. The boys looked strong, healthy and happy.

"Awfully glad to meet you," said the father. "My name is Egglebert Lillienthal Smith III, but you can call me Richard. This is my wife Althea, and my sons X, Y, and Z. We're talkers."

Eloise was even more impressed now. She knew that humans came in many different kinds and that talkers were among the most powerful and important of all.

"Glad to meet you," said Eloise. She tried to curtsy, but not having had much practice, she fell flat on her face. A strong hand helped her up from the ground. She looked up and saw that it was X, the oldest and tallest of the Smith boys. "Thanks," she said, her face pale with embarrassment.

"I say, I do hope it's no problem putting our house up here. We can move it if—," Mr. Smith said.

"Oh no," said Eloise. "You can build anywhere, just not on top of anyone else's place."

"We'd never do that. It sounds uncomfortable," Mrs. Smith said. Eloise could not tell if she was joking. "Where do you come from?" Gartrude asked.

"You ask, 'Where do we come from?'" Mr. Smith replied. He drew a deep breath. "We come from near and we come from far. We travel the galaxy, from one end to the other. No planet is too small or too humble to escape our notice. Take Planet Wampetter for example. For too long your planet has been deprived of the glories of intergalactic commerce and the rest of the galaxy has been deprived of the riches of your world. And so we have come, as facilitators of fun, prophets of profit, developers of delight."

He paused for a moment and it seemed as if he were finished, but he was not.

"You ask, 'But why? Why leave the comforts of home and journey across the vacuum of space, risking death, bad reception and yucky food?' Well, my Daddy explained it to me when I was a little boy. We were out behind the barn one summer's night, gazing up at the starry sky and he said, 'Son. It may look pretty, but there's a lot of places up there that need improvement.' We've come here to make improvements. We're going to improve everything!"

"Everything?" Eloise asked.

"Everything that needs improvement."

Eloise could only nod in astonishment. She had never heard such talk before, except on the bigscreen. Wampetters are plain creatures, given to plain talk, while talkers are, well, talkers.

"You want to see the neighborhood?" Gartrude asked the boys.

The boys glanced hopefully at their parents.

"That's fine," Mrs. Smith said. Just make sure you have your Rescue-Paks."

"Of course, Mom," X said.

"Sure thing," Y added.

"Never leave home without it," Z said.

And so they ran off, the boys loping over the hills and the girls pounding after them, until they all flopped down beneath a brindlebrush tree that stood in the middle of a broad meadow.

"Why do you have letters for names?" Eloise asked. "I mean, if you don't mind saying."

"No problem," said Z.

"No skin off my teeth," Y added.

"Sure," said X. "Every talker child starts out with a letter of the alphabet and then when you grow up, you get a real name. You have to do something to earn a name, you don't just get one because you're there. If you do something really great we say, 'That's worth a name.' I'm almost old enough to get one."

"That's interesting," Eloise said.

"Let's play Hide and Get Lost," Gartrude suggested.

"Gar—," Eloise protested.

"Sounds good," said Z.

"Righteous," added Y.

"Count me in," said X

Gartrude leapt to her feet. "I'm it. Count to a hundred." She ran off at top speed. She was at that age when she would do just about anything to impress other kids, especially older kids, especially older kids from another planet. She was determined to hide somewhere they would never find her. When they gave up looking for her she would burst from her hiding place and they would all want to know how she did it but she would not say, not unless they begged.

She ran through a thicket of spoogplant, splashed across a wide stream and clambered up the rocky bank on the other side. Soon she reached the Quake Zone. Her parents, Albert and Berthe, had warned her

many times not to wander into the Quake Zone, but Gartrude was feeling daring, and besides she would be very careful and only go in a little ways. Treading lightly, she crossed the uneven ground until she found a perfect hiding spot behind a big rock. She settled down to wait. As it turned out, she did not have to wait long.

She heard a distant rumbling, like a train coming from far away. She looked around but saw nothing unusual. The noise grew louder. She thought it might be a space ship but the sky was clear. Suddenly the ground opened beneath her feet and she fell straight

down. She fell deeper and deeper into the crevice, then suddenly stopped. She was wedged in around her tummy, like a cork in a bottle. Like all wampetters she had a tough skin and plenty of cushioning around the middle, so she was not hurt, but she was stuck. She cried out but no one heard. Meanwhile the bright patch of sky at the top of the hole gradually changed from pink to deep purple. She shivered as the day cooled.

Gartrude was scared. She promised that she would never run off again, that she would always obey her parents. She promised that she would eat all her porridge for breakfast and never take a bath just before the family was supposed to go out dirty for a special event. Oh, she would be so good, everyone would see, if only she could get out of this hole. She just wanted to see her sister and her parents and her house again. The wind howled. Tears ran down her cheeks.

Meanwhile the Smith boys had lost interest in the game and gone home. Only Eloise kept searching. She knew that even if Gartrude had found the perfect hiding place, she would not be able to sit still for this long. She would have come rushing out on some excuse long before—unless something happened. Eloise worried that it was something bad.

Eloise told her mother, Berthe, and Berthe told Albert and they all searched for Gartrude. Eloise was looking in the forest when she came across X reading a book beneath a waytall tree.

"Are you still playing?" he asked.

"I'm afraid Gartrude's really lost," Eloise said.

"Doesn't she have a Rescue-Pak?" X asked.

"No."

"Well she should," said X. "It should be required on a planet like this."

"I'm so worried about her."

"I can find her if you want," X said.

"Oh, please."

"No problem. I'll use my Pak." X unstrapped from his waist a small black object, about the size of a candy bar, which expanded into a large cube. X spoke into one end: "Rescue mission, search mode, target Gartrude, wampetter." He turned to Eloise. "Speak into this and tell it what your sister's like—how she might be recognized."

"Well, she's a wampetter, orange and plump, five years old, with bright green eyes, a big mouth and little ears. She's always getting into trouble because she doesn't listen to anyone and just does what she wants and I'm really afraid that maybe she went into the Quake Zone because that's so dangerous and no one can go in there except if you do you can get hurt."

X pressed a series of buttons on the cube. It hummed in response and then with a pffft sound, a small hatch opened at the top and a tiny insect-like object flew out. It hovered above them a few seconds, and then flew off.

"That's the probe. We just watch here to see if it finds anything." X pointed to a screen that appeared on one side of the cube.

Eloise called to her parents and they all huddled close to the screen, their fingers and toes and eyes crossed, hoping against hope that Gartrude might be found.

A buzzing sound began, followed by a whooping

siren. A message appeared: SUBJECT FOUND. The screen flashed a picture of Gartrude in her hole in the Quake Zone.

"Oh my baby!" Berthe cried.

"My little G!" Albert screamed.

"What can we do?" Eloise shrieked.

"Nothing. It's all taken care of," X said.

Gartrude was afraid of the dark insect-like thing that buzzed around her head. She thought it was going to bite her and so she tried to bite it first. As a

result, it took several minutes for the probe to complete the rescue preliminaries. Soon Gartrude noticed that there were little strings all over her clothes attached to a big white thing over her head that looked just like a balloon. In fact it was a balloon. As the balloon filled, the strings tugged her upwards. When she let out her breath in a great sigh, Gartrude was lifted free. The balloon soared into the sky and Gartrude soared with it, out of the hole and across the Quake Zone and straight back to her home.

She looked down and there they were: her parents and sister and all the Smiths, yelling and pointing.

She yelled back: "Look at me, I'm flying, I'm flying. And you couldn't find me!" But then she remembered how scared she had been and decided not to say anything more about the game. She landed gently in front of her sister. There followed several minutes of hugs and cries and foot-stomping. Gartrude promised never, ever to disobey her parents, and all the Tubs thanked X for his help.

Finally Albert said it was time to go home. Gartrude nodded and leaned her head against her father's tummy. "Thanks again for everything," Albert told the Smiths. "If there's anything we can do for you—"

"Well, we'd be delighted if you could come to dinner tomorrow," Mr. Smith said. "We have a great deal to discuss."

"We wouldn't miss it for anything," Albert said.

Eloise gave X a shy wave. He nodded and smiled back at her. As they walked home she decided she liked him. She was already looking forward to dinner at the Smith house.

CHAPTER TWO

Promises of Plenty

The following day the Tub family faced a crisis. It reduced Eloise to tears and Gartrude to screeching. Even Berthe moaned. The situation had never come up before.What does a wampetter wear to dinner at a talker's house?

When the time came to leave for the Smith's house, only Albert was ready. He was clad in his usual party outfit: shocking pink shoes, plastic see-through pants, purple and gold polka dot underwear, a red striped shirt, flower print tie and green plaid jacket.

"Oh, you look so handsome," Berthe declared. "I love the way those colors clash." They nuzzled noses. "But look at me. I'm so thin!"

"You look great," Albert said. "And you know humans think it's better to be slender."

"You're right!" she chirped. "They'll think I'm fashionable."

Albert went to check on his daughters' progress.

Their room was strewn with clothes. There were dresses on the bed, skirts and blouses covered the floor. There were stockings draped over the windows, shoes hooked on the doorknob and underwear under the bed. The girls gazed forlornly at their father.

"I don't have any clothes," Eloise complained.

"Me too," said Gartrude.

Albert shook his head. He waded into the room and made some suggestions. Soon everyone was dressed and headed for the Smiths.

"Welcome to our humble home," said Mr. Smith, opening the great front door. "Please, come in."

The first thing Eloise noticed was the quiet. It was not a hard quiet like a city street late at night, but a soft quiet, like a meadow at sunset, before the birds begin their songs, when the little creatures, the rodents and insects tread softly in the underbrush as they hurry home and the wind sighs in the grasses.

"It sounds so peaceful," Eloise said.

"It's the latest stuff from Aurelia," X said. Aurelia was the planet famous throughout the galaxy for its beautiful sounds.

Each room had its own scent. One smelled of wild flowers, another of cedar trees, and another of a forest after a spring rain.

"Look at this everybody!" Gartrude yelled to the others. "You won't believe it."

"This is the sea room," Mrs. Smith explained as they entered the large blue and green chamber.

One wall of the room was made of glass and

revealed an enormous aquarium where creatures of all colors and sizes swam.

"But that's, that's—" gasped Albert, pointing at the tank.

A large pale creature that looked a great deal like young Z wearing breathing gear pressed its nose flat against the glass and stuck out its tongue at them.

"Come on out Z," Mrs. Smith yelled. "We have company."

"It's like having the ocean in your house," Eloise said, amazed.

"It's no big deal," said X.

Albert, though, could barely take his eyes off the tank. In a lifetime of fishing he had never seen so many different creatures close up.

X and Y took the girls to their Simulation Chambers—rooms which could recreate virtually any environment in the universe. X showed Eloise his fighter ship simulation, which was interesting for a while. Then Y took them to the mountains of Karnak where they took turns shooting at wild Beestiavs who tried to devour them. Gartrude nearly lost her big toe to one particularly ferocious beast. Fortunately it was just a simulation. Then Mrs. Smith called them down for dinner.

They entered an elegant dining room where a long marble table stood laden with exotic foods. By this time the Tubs were speechless, even Gartrude, who they sometimes joked had never stopped talking since she learned how. They sat down to eat. There was fresh shrimp from Planet Ulgre and delicate pastries from Paris and much, much more. It was the best meal that anyone could remember, and for a wampetter, who can usually remember every meal she's eaten for months and months, that is high praise. The Tubs had seconds on everything and went back for thirds and sometimes fourths of especially delectable items.

When no one could eat a bite more, Mr. Smith stood up from his place at the head of the table. "As you may know, there comes a time in every young talker's life when he or she receives a full name. We never know in advance when this will

happen. For our dear son X, it happened yesterday." Mr. Smith waved his hand and the lights in the room dimmed, except a bright white spotlight that shone on X. "In the best tradition of our people and our land, X came to the rescue of a tike in trouble, a damsel in distress, a Gartrude in grievous circumstances, namely a tight spot in the Quake Zone. Son, please stand up."

X stood up and faced his father.

"For your sound judgment, compassion and courage, it is my honor as your father to name you:"

He paused. Eloise held her breath with excitement. Gartrude's teeth chattered and her ears wiggled.

"We name you—" his father paused again.

"We name you—Bill," his father intoned.

"Bill?" asked Albert.

"Bill?" exclaimed Eloise.

"Bill?" cried X in astonishment.

"Certainly," Mrs. Smith said. "Bill is a fine old talker name. You should be proud to bear it."

"Well, I guess it's better than X," Bill said.

"Darn right," Mr. Smith declared. He turned to his wife. "Dear, would you tell our guests about the rest of the ceremony?"

"Certainly," Mrs. Smith replied. "According to tradition, the family always presents gifts to those who come to a naming. The boys have already received theirs. Now we would like to give you something."

"Yeah!" said Albert and Berthe in unison.

"Whoopee!" added Gartrude and Eloise.

Wampetters love presents and believe you should express great enthusiasm for them before you find out what they are. That way you can thank the present-giver for the most wonderful thing you can imagine. After you see what it is, you may be disappointed.

Each of the Tubs thought about all the wonderful things they had seen in the Smith house, and which they would like to take home.

"Please come outside," Mrs. Smith said.

They followed her out the back door.

"Da dah!" she said, with a great flourish. She stood

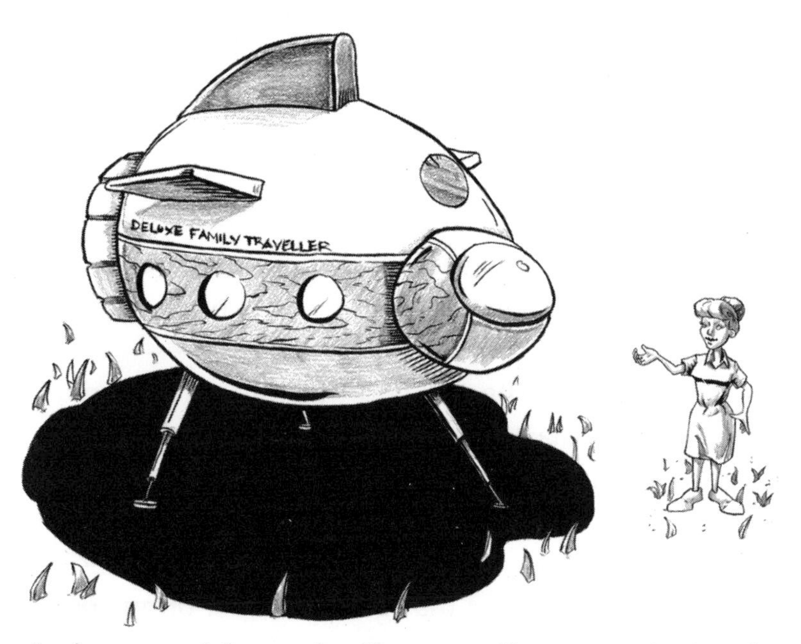

before a deluxe family traveller—a vehicle for planetary and space travel. This was one of the newest models, the kind that human families took on jaunts "from here to there, whether it's across the street or across the universe," as the song went on the bigscreen ad. From the ads the Tubs knew it held eight in comfort and could circle the planet in half a day.

"Are we going somewhere?" Eloise asked finally.

"That's up to you," Mr. Smith replied.

"I want my present!" Gartrude demanded. "You promised."

"Gartrude!" her father scolded.

"We're sorry we could only give you one thing but—" Mr. Smith began.

"That's not fair, you said we'd all get something," Gartrude interrupted. She began to cry and whine at the same time, an awful combination.

"You'd better explain," Mr. Smith told his wife.

"Certainly. Our wampetter friends—this traveller—this brand new Super X Time-Shifter Lightning Model 7 is all yours."

Gartrude sprang to her feet. The whites of Albert's eyes grew to the size of hard-boiled eggs. Berthe slapped her hands on her cheeks. Eloise bit her elbows with excitement.

Could it really be true? Could this extraordinary piece of intergalactic machinery really be theirs? No longer would they have to put up with the ancient family traveller that always stalled on take-off, with a radio you had to kick to change channels and a navigational computer that got them lost on purpose to show them who was really in charge. Now they would be able to take luggage with them on trips instead of just a small paperback, a change of underwear and a toothbrush—the only things they could fit in the old machine besides themselves. Could it be true?

"But it's so—" Eloise couldn't even finish the thought.

"We could never—" Berthe tried.

"Not in a thousand years—" Albert offered.

"It costs too much," said Gartrude. Sometimes it's best to just come right out and say it.

"Oh, no," Mr. Smith said. "Not at all. It's free. Can't get any cheaper than that, can you?"

"But it's too much," Berthe said. "You'll be poor."

The Smiths all laughed. Mrs. Smith put a hand on Berthe's broad shoulder. "Don't you worry about us. Consider this a gift from our people to yours, a sign of our friendship, a symbol of what planetary development will mean."

"Well thank you," said Berthe.

"A thousand times, thanks," said Albert. "Now we must give you something in return."

The Tub family looked at each other, all thinking the same thing: What could they ever give this family that seemed to have everything?

"Maybe they'd like some brontosaurus mud pie," Gartrude suggested. She turned to the Smiths. "I baked some specially this afternoon."

Everyone laughed.

"Please, you must feel no obligation," Mr. Smith said.

"No, we must," Albert replied. "I have an idea. Tubs, come close." He gathered the family around him and whispered something, to which they all nodded in agreement.

"Our gift is a song," Albert told the Smiths. "This song has been in my family for ten generations. It

comes from a time when we lived in the mountains."

The family stood in a semi-circle, heads bowed, waiting for Albert to begin.

As you already know, wampetters are plain talkers, and as you may have heard, they are clumsy dancers, prone to falling down. Wampetters are wonderful singers, though. Their traditional songs are called "airs of the wind" for they open and close with a rushing sound like the wind over the prairie.

Albert began, in a voice broad and smooth:

Father wind, mother wind
Where have you gone?
Father wind, mother wind
Where have you gone?

Berthe joined him in the next verse, adding a higher, reedy voice to the song:

High in the crags where the sharp birds nest,
Down in the valleys where the meadows sway,
Over hard plains and frosted seas
You bring warm to the cold,
And cool to the hot;
Drink to the thirsty;
And dry to the wet;
Seeds to the earth
And earth to the seeds.

Their voices trailed off into the night air. Two breaths later Eloise and Gartrude sang in voices high and sad:

Father wind, mother wind
Where have you flown?
The land lies parched and the air hangs still
Father wind, mother wind,
Where do you dance?
Father wind, mother wind
What have we done?

The whole family sang the last verse. Their four voices blended together into a powerful choir:

The treetops stir, a breath in our face,
Dark shapes above, the tang of wet earth
A rush of clouds, a sweep of rain
Father wind, home again;
Mother wind, home again.
Our thanks. A thousand times, thanks.

After a moment's silence, the Smiths burst into applause. The Tubs bowed their heads in modest appreciation.

"Outrageous," said Bill.

"Oh yeah," said Y.

"Ditto," said Z.

"You know, this is why we travel across the great vacuum of space," Mr. Smith said. "The galaxy has no conception of the talent here. With your permission, I would like to make a test recording of your singing, just a little something I could show around the industry. I have a pretty good sense for the market for these things. I think this could be very profitable for you. And you would bring such beauty to the lives of others. The depth of feeling—oh, it's stunning."

"Thank you for your kind words, but this was our gift," Albert said.

"Oh, I realize that, and believe me I am grateful, but you are too modest if you think others wouldn't love it as well," Mr. Smiths said.

"No, thank you," Albert said firmly. The other

wampetters looked away, embarrassed.

Mr. Smith laughed. "You don't understand. You're sitting on a gold mine here. Forget about the others—the Trapp Family singers, the Jacksons, the Osmonds, they're nothing compared to you. You could put out disks of the songs, do a tour, a couple of bigscreen shows, maybe a series. I can see a theme park on traditional culture, with concerts every night. You could make millions, maybe more. Oh, you just can't turn your back on something like this, not without giving it some thought at least. Will you at least think about it? You don't have to give me an answer now. Just think about it, okay?"

A long silence followed. Albert's face turned dark. "We gave this song to you and your family," he said in a hard voice. "You will have it always in your memory. What you ask for now you can never have. It's not ours to give, not that way. Please, Mr. Smith. Never mention this again, or it will be the last words exchanged between us."

Mr. Smith was about to respond, but his wife raised a finger in warning and he simply smiled.

"We apologize if we offended you," Mrs. Smith said. "We will not speak of it again."

Gartrude and Eloise were so pleased at this that they clapped and the others laughed.

Bill and Y closed out the festivities with a traditional talker child's song, which they sang loud and out of tune to the delight of both families. The Tubs clambered aboard their new traveller and took it for a brief jaunt around the neighborhood before landing in their front yard. The machine was so wonderful that no one wanted to get out. When Eloise and Gartrude were finally tucked in bed, they snuck a last look at the traveller from their bedroom window.

"I can't believe it," Eloise said.

"Yeah," said Gartrude. "We're rich."

"You think so?"

"We will be if we have dinner there enough," Gartrude said.

"Oh Gartrude, they're not going to give us a new traveller every time we go to dinner."

"They could," her little sister insisted.

"No, this was special. Really special," Eloise said.

CHAPTER THREE
Changes

The beautiful Hannah was not happy. No, she was not pleased. As she stomped down the hallway toward the set, eyes ablaze, lips curling back from her teeth in an awful grimace, reaching with long-nailed fingers like a predator about to pounce on its prey, she did not look at all like the warm, ever-cheerful director of an orphanage, the part she played in her bigscreen series, *A Family Wampetter.*

"Where are they?" she screamed. "Where are those

fat little pumpkins? This time I'm going to chop them up into little bits and—"

"Hannah, my beautiful Hannah," said Sid, the director of the show. "What can be the matter?"

"You know what those little wampetters did? They put ants in my special face cream, the kind made out of rare baby flowers."

"I'm so sorry," said Sid. "I'm sure they didn't realize how important your face cream is to you.You know how they like to joke."

"I'll teach them about joking. I'll catch them and torture them with my bare hands, very slowly. Then I'll blow up the whole planet. I'll erase wampetters from galactic existence. I'll—"

"Hannah, please, someone will hear."

"I don't care. Wampetters, beware. The wrath of Hannah will be on your heads!"

"Uh, Hannah, this is Richard Smith—the gentleman I was telling you about? He's head of the Planetary Development Commission."

"Development of what?" Hannah asked sharply.

"Why Planet Wampetter, of course," Mr. Smith said.

"You ought to just blow the place up," Hannah responded.

Mr. Smith chuckled. "You have quite a sense of humor."

"Hannah," Sid said gently. "Mr. Smith is the one who might be interested in backing a new series for you—one that shoots on another planet."

Hannah's personality underwent a remarkable

transformation. She smiled sweetly and shook out her hair. She kissed Mr. Smith on the cheek. He flushed bright pink with her sudden attention. She took his hand. "I'm so sorry Richard, I hope I can call you that. Our shooting schedule's been impossible. I must look a total wreck."

"You look beautiful; one of the most gorgeous creatures in the galaxy," Mr. Smith responded.

Hannah's smile brightened further. Right then it seemed the old saying was true, that when the beautiful Hannah smiled, the galaxy smiled with her. She was one of the most attractive of her kind, the beautiful people. She had thick, curly yellow-pink hair and green eyes like the sea in the tropics, and a slender figure with graceful, generous curves.

"We wonder if you would do this public service announcement for us," Mr. Smith said. "It'll only take a couple of minutes and I, and the Commission, would be forever grateful. We have everything set up over here."

"Just tell me what you'd like," Hannah said.

Three days later the Tub family gathered around their bigscreen. Eloise and Gartrude bounced up and down with anticipation; Albert and Berthe affectionately poked each other in the tummy, a favorite habit of theirs. They anxiously awaited the start of their favorite show, the intergalactic hit, *A Family Wampetter,* starring the beautiful Hannah. They also wanted to hear the important announcement that everyone was talking about.

"I think Hannah's getting married," Gartrude said.

"She said she'd never get married again," Eloise said. "And she's already tried it three times."

"But maybe she met Mr. Beautiful," Gartrude argued.

"Bill told me it has to do with the future of the planet," Eloise said quietly.

They all turned to her. "The future of the planet!" they said in unison.

"Look! It's Mr. Smith!" Albert yelled, pointing at the bigscreen.

"Good evening wampetters. My name is Richard

Smith and I have come from a long way away to help your planet. I would like you to listen carefully to the following message from a very good friend of mine—and yours—the beautiful Hannah."

Hannah appeared, looking more radiant than ever, seated in the familiar living room of the orphanage, surrounded by her little orphan wampetters on the show. "Hello friends. How are you tonight? I'm here with my family, to talk to you about something important. It won't take long but it is awfully important, so I hope you'll pay close attention."

The Tubs edged closer to the bigscreen. Albert had to pull Gartrude back because her nose was pressed flat against the screen.

"For as long as I have been here I have felt a special bond with all wampetters," Hannah said. "I love your quick-blooming smiles and your innocence, your sense of humor and your caring. And I love this planet. It has such unspoiled beauty. I would never want anything bad to happen to any living thing on this planet. This comes straight from the heart." She touched her fingertips to the center of her chest.

"It's because I love this place so much that I have to tell you about the problems I see. I see too many adult wampetters without jobs. I see a planet cut off from the galactic mainstream, without any chance to participate in the wonderful cultural exchanges that go on between so many planets. I see families without enough food to eat, or decent clothes to wear. And I see wampetters suffering with medical conditions that could be cured."

Here she paused and turned to the young wampetters with her. "Little Jeen, would you come here?"

A small boy wampetter felt his way over to Hannah and curled up in her lap.

"You all know my little Jeen. I know he has a special place in your heart, as he does in mine, because many of you have written to tell me. Little Jeen was born blind. Of course that's never stopped him. He plays like all the other little wampetters. He laughs and cries right along with the rest. But he's never seen the spring flowers, or a sunset or even my face. And you know what? He could. On my home planet doctors have devised an operation which could cure little Jeen, could give him sight. It's a miracle of modern medicine, but they can do it. Because on my home planet we have the most advanced medical technology, the best doctors and hospitals. Sadly, there is no way that this operation could be done on Planet Wampetter.

"Some time ago I asked little Jeen if I couldn't just take him home with me for a while and have the operation done, but you know what he told me? You know what this child said? He told me that he didn't want to go unless every other wampetter could go. Because he knows there are thousands of other little boy and girl wampetters who also need operations that can't be done on this planet. And he doesn't want to be singled out for special favors, just because he's on a bigscreen show.

"I told him I understood. But isn't it a shame? Can't we do something about this, something to give little Jeen and all the other little ones a chance to see, a chance to lead full and happy and normal lives?" She sighed and smoothed little Jeen's hair.

"I'm telling you this because there is something you can do to help. A group of people have recently come to this planet with some very big and exciting plans. They want to make it so that no wampetter will ever go without the very best in health care. I'm asking you tonight if you won't help them."

"They'll be coming to your door in the next few days with a piece of paper called a Consent to Develop. You should read it carefully and ask any questions you want. It gives them permission to do the fine work that they need to do. Won't you sign? Won't you help little Jeen see?"

"Yes!" yelled all of the Tubs in unison. Indeed, all over the planet, wampetters shouted their agreement. They wanted to help.

Within a week the Tubs had their signed Consent hung over the mantel. Festooned with blue and red ribbons and the big gold seal of the Intergalactic International Very Official United Federation of Creatures, Planets and Other Bits and Pieces of Space Matter—more commonly known as the Association—the document declared the consent of the Tub family to a development plan by the Planet Wampetter Development Commission.

Nearly everyone signed. A few wampetters refused because they did not understand or were generally negative, but everyone else thought it was a great idea. Within two weeks the Commission had enough signatures to start development.

All over the planet, wampetters talked about the changes that development would bring. There was talk of a new traveller in every yard, candy in every pocket and toothpaste on every sink. (For reasons no one has ever fully understood, there has long been a shortage of toothpaste on Planet Wampetter. Some scientists theorize it is because wampetters like to squeeze the toothpaste tubes with their feet, resulting in a considerable waste and mess—although as a result no wampetter has ever gotten a cavity in their toes, which should count for something.) The Tubs became famous in their sector for their new traveller and spent long days showing it off to friends, neighbors and acquaintances.

The Tubs were enthusiastic supporters of development and anxiously followed the news of its progress. They were especially anxious to hear about little Jeen's operation. Little Jeen was their favorite character—after the beautiful Hannah of course—on their favorite show and they wanted to be sure he was okay.

One day Eloise asked Bill about it. "Do you know about little Jeen? Can he see yet?"

Bill laughed. Then he became serious. "Sorry. I know you're worried about him. He just left for the operation. It'll be on the bigscreen pretty soon. Don't worry. You'll hear all about it."

"That's great," Eloise said.

"Yeah," he replied.

"It's so exciting," Eloise said. "All the changes I mean."

"I guess. We do this all the time you know."

"Really?"

"Sure. This is my dad's thirtieth planet."

"Wow."

"And he's in charge of everything. Sometimes he asks me what I think."

"Isn't that kind of scary?"

"Nah. You'd be surprised how simple it is. Well, gotta run. See you around."

"Okay."

Bill ran into the house. Eloise wished they could play together more.

Every week seemed to bring another big change.

First came the IDs. The Development Commission said that everyone had to go to their post office and have a picture taken and get a number for an ID. Once you got the ID you were supposed to hang it around your neck. It was for identification, but no one understood why it was needed. Not that many folks forget who they are during the average day. The wampetters who were in charge of the project tried to keep everything straight, but a lot of the young wampetters had their pictures taken three times and then the numbers got a little mixed up. As a result, there were some surprises when the IDs came in the mail. Eloise was so upset she locked herself in her room for an hour. The ID with her name on it had the picture of a grizzled old wampetter without any teeth. In fact, very few IDs had the right pictures or numbers. Gartrude's ID showed a very pretty girl wampetter about ten years older than she; Albert and

Berthe's had the right pictures but the wrong names. The joke was that with the IDs no one knew who they were any more.

The next event was the job fair, announced on *A Family Wampetter.* If it was possible, the show had become even more popular. At exactly 8 p.m. on Thursday all across the planet, wampetters dropped everything to watch the show. Now they watched not just for the beautiful Hannah and the high jinks of her high-spirited wampetter clan, they also watched for announcements by Mr. Smith.

"My friends and global neighbors," Mr. Smith said. "Have you dreamed of a new traveller, a real galactic-

class machine with plush seats and fully automatic controls? Have you ever wanted to visit distant planets, to bathe in the oceans of Resark or ski the mountains of Baroo? Well you can make those dreams come true with a new job from the Development Commission. Come on down to the job fair. If you have an old job, turn it in for a new one. If you don't have a job, see what we can offer you. This is your chance to make real money. The fair opens tomorrow."

"Oh, can we go? Please Mom, please Dad," Eloise begged.

"Tomorrow," Gartrude urged.

"Children. You both have school tomorrow."

"But this is more important," Eloise said. "Everything's changing and we have to be part of it. We have to get there right at the beginning before all the best jobs are taken."

Berthe looked at Albert. "Maybe we should," she said.

"Okay," Albert said. Then he walked out of the house.

"What's wrong with Dad?" Eloise asked her mother.

"Your father is a very talented journalist. You know his column, "Something Fishy," is one of the most-read features in the *Daily News of Yesterday.* He's very proud of his work as a fishing correspondent. It's hard to give that up."

"Won't they let him keep it?"

"I don't know dear."

"Then he should just drop us off. We can get new

jobs and he can keep his old one."

"I agree. But he wants to be part of the planet's improvement. He wants to do his part."

The next day they arose when the sky was still a deep purple and the moons of Budeel and Ah shone like pale yellow bananas in the east. The morning air was sharp with cold as they clambered aboard the traveller. Albert whispered instructions to the ship's navigator and they were off, headed west. As the sun broke over the Talen Mountains, its crimson light seemed to set the plains afire. To everyone's surprise, Albert broke into song. They all joined in to sing that old wampetter classic, "A Hundred Bottles of Beer in the Refrigerator and A Lot More in the Oven." You may have heard a song like this, but this is the original.

"So, what do you want to do for Planet Wampetter my little G?" Albert asked Gartrude when they finished the song.

"I want to drive one of those really really really big dump trucks, the kind with wheels higher than our house, that can run over anything. Or one of those bulldozer machines that squash mountains," she said cheerfully. "Or I'd like to drive a tank and blast things. Boom, boom. Do you think they'll have tanks?"

"I certainly hope not. You know we don't approve of guns," Albert said.

"Darn!" Gartrude exclaimed.

"I'm going to be a scientist," Eloise announced. I'm going to find out the secret of the Big Poof and win the Dumb Bell Prize."

"The Big Poof?" asked Gartrude.

"Yes. It's how the universe started."

"Boring," Gartrude said, sticking out her tongue.

"I've never heard of this Dumb Bell Prize," Albert said.

"It's the big prize for scientists all over the galaxy," Eloise said. "No one from Planet Wampetter has ever been considered for it. It was started by this really rich family that was really dumb. That's why they call it the Dumb Bell Prize."

"What about you dear?" Albert asked Berthe.

"I'm going to be an intergalactic trip coordinator if I can. Something where I work with intelligent creatures."

The traveller began the descent toward the huge tents where the job fair was held. Eloise pulled on her fingers. She wondered, "What would happen next? Would this really be the most important thing that ever happened to them, the way Mr. Smith had said?"

The Tubs spent a long morning in the tent filling out paperwork, posing for pictures, answering questions and taking tests. When they finally emerged at midday, they were famished, and rushed to the food vendors who had set up nearby. They quickly stuffed their faces with food.

"I'm woann we a webawamp," Gartrude said, her mouth full of potatoes and lemon gravy.

"What?" Berthe asked.

"I'm going to be a celebrant!" Gartrude shouted, spraying food everywhere.

"You know on other planets it's bad manners to

talk with food in your mouth," Berthe said.

"Who cares," Gartrude said, stuffing a plum in her mouth. "My job is to be authentic."

"Authentic?" Albert asked.

"Yup. An authentic wampetter so visitors know what we're like."

"You don't have to sing do you?" Albert asked.

"No Dad. We just dance around and give directions."

"But you're always getting lost yourself," Eloise observed.

"I haven't gotten lost once this week!" Gartrude protested.

"Well, I have a position working in a brand new restaurant, a very fancy one, catering to foreign visitors. I have to get all kinds of special training," Berthe said proudly.

"That's wonderful," Albert said, and gave her a big hug and smooch.

"It's not fair!" Eloise protested. "They said I had to stay in school."

"That's so you can be a scientist when you grow up," Albert said.

"What about you Dad?" Eloise asked.

"I turned in my old job. No more fishing correspondent for the *Daily News of Yesterday.* I don't have anything else, but the Development Commission will pay me just the same until they find something that's right for me."

"Sounds like they're saving you for something really special," Berthe said.

Albert nodded and poked at his food. He had barely eaten anything.

In the next few weeks Albert grew quiet. He stopped going fishing because his favorite fishing spots had been fenced off and posted with No Trespassing signs. Day after day he sat in his comfortable chair by the front window and looked out, waiting for the phone to ring. It did sometimes, but it was never for him. He ate little and grew thin. Everyone tried to cheer him up. Gartrude did tricks and Eloise read him stories and Berthe sang him songs. He always smiled and said thanks and he was never grumpy or sharp, but the sadness remained.

The next change came about three weeks later. Eloise returned home from school to find everyone frantically packing.

"We're moving!" Gartrude shouted. "We're going to the city!"

"Why, Mom?" Eloise asked Berthe.

"Mr. Smith says they're doing a fancy housing development. With a golf course, whatever that is."

"What about the Smiths? Do they have to move?" Eloise said.

"I don't think so," Berthe said. "You better get started, we don't have much time."

Within an hour they had all of their furniture and possessions packed in the traveller. Then came the machines. There was a huge bulldozer that stood twice as high as the house and a dump truck that was even bigger. Bill joined them as the bulldozer approached the Tub house.

"We always said it was too small," Berthe said.

"And the roof leaks," Eloise said.

"And the front door sticks," Gartrude added.

But when the bulldozer crashed through the house like a child smashing a mud pie, they all cried out. It had been their home for many years.

"I'm never going to do that," Gartrude announced. "I want to drive a big truck but I don't want to smash anybody's house. I don't like that."

"Neither do I," said Albert.

"You'll get a new house," Bill said. "It'll be even better."

"But we don't want a new house," said Gartrude.

"Can we come back and visit?" Eloise asked.

"Yes. You have to," Bill said.

The Tubs moved to an apartment in a new building in the city. It actually had more room than the old house and more modern conveniences, but Eloise still missed the old place.

For a while everything seemed okay. Albert fixed up the new apartment. Berthe started her job training and on Saturdays Gartrude took classes in celebrating. Then Albert starting buying things.

The Development Commission had opened huge new stores in the city which sold all of the wonders of the galaxy on credit, meaning you could buy now and pay later. Every day Albert came home with a big package.

He bought a combination washing machine and microwave, which sounded like a good idea except it made food taste like dirty clothes and left food stains on the clean laundry. He bought a fancy coffee grinder although they didn't drink coffee and an automatic rug shampooer even though they had no rugs. Albert said they would be ready if someone wanted coffee or if they bought a rug. Every night the family gathered in the living room and Albert asked Berthe or one of the girls to open his latest present. He never bought anything for himself. Later Berthe collected the packages and stacked them in the spare bedroom.

One morning when Albert had gone out for a walk, Eloise asked her mom: "Why does Dad buy all those things nobody wants?"

"He's just trying to make us happy," Berthe said. "Don't you think that's nice?"

"It seems kind of expensive."

"Don't worry, dear," her mother said. "If it was a problem the stores wouldn't let him take the things home."

"I guess."

"Pretty soon they'll call with his new job."

Eloise nodded.

But the Development Commission did not call and Albert started talking about how they should buy a second traveller. He brought home pictures of the latest models and asked for their opinions. No one knew what to say.

The next morning as Eloise waited for her school bus she made a decision. She told her friends she had forgotten something at home and ran around the block. Then she set off for her old neighborhood. She needed to see Bill. Maybe he would know what to do. Maybe his father could get a job for Albert.

Her heart thumped hard as she set off through the city. She did not have permission and did not know how long it would take to walk. She knew the way though, and knew she had to do something.

She started out in the eastern sector of Foom, the largest city on the planet. She soon entered the business section, with its characteristic trapezoidal buildings. The sidewalks were crowded with street vendors and workers hurrying to and from their jobs. She passed a street full of bouncing parlors, places where wampetters could go to leap on a trampoline, a popular form of relaxation. She loved the way you could see creatures fly into the air above the buildings and then disappear. There are no roofs on bouncing parlors.

She walked through a run-down neighborhood

where wampetters with tired eyes and thin bodies leaned against dirty buildings. Twice she scurried into doorways when she heard police sirens. In recent months there had been more fights and reports of stealing, so the city's few police kept very busy.

At noon she sat beneath a yarwaa tree in a park on the outskirts of the city and ate the lunch her mother had packed for her. She was halfway there. If she hurried she might make it to the Smiths before dark. But how would she ever get home? She decided not to think about it.

The sun was low in the sky when, dragging her feet in the dust, she climbed the last hill to their old neighborhood. At the top she stopped and looked around. The only thing the bulldozers had left standing was the Smith's house.

She rang the bell three times but there was no answer. She knocked on the door—nothing. There were no lights on. Where could they be? She stifled a moan. "What if they've moved?" she thought. Maybe they've gone off to another planet. I'm too late. She could take it no more. She burst out crying.

"You know we don't allow crying here." The voice was deep and stern, but somehow it did not scare Eloise. She turned around. A tall man with silver hair leaned over her. He wore the strangest cap she had ever seen, a red beanie with two enormous propellers that twirled in opposite directions.

"I'm sorry. I'm looking for Bill Smith," Eloise said. "He used to live here. Do you know where he went? I have to find him. It's very important."

"Bill? Bill Smith you say? Yes, I recollect a Bill

Smith. In fact, he's my nephew. In fact, he lives right here. They've just gone out to do some errands."

"Oh," she said.

"I'm his Uncle Rudy. I've just come to visit. And I'll bet you're Eloise."

"How did you know?"

"Because Bill has told me all about you and your family. He rescued your sister, or so he says."

"He did. She was lost in the Quake Zone."

"Dear me. Sounds awful. I'm sorry no one was here to greet you. I like to go out for a walk around sunset. Now come on in out of the cold. I bet you'd like something to eat and drink."

She allowed herself a little nod.

Uncle Rudy led her inside. He called her parents to

let them know where she was and that he would give her a ride home. Then he fixed her a small snack: a pint of milk, a pitcher of lemonade, three sandwiches, two apples, a large piece of pie and a small, well, kind of a medium size slice of chocolate cake. When she was finished she told Uncle Rudy about her father's problem. Uncle Rudy listened carefully, his chin propped in his gnarled hands. Occasionally he leaned back and flicked one of the propellers on his hat.

"Well, we'll just have to do something about all this," he said when she had explained everything.

"Really? Do you mean that? Can you get my dad a job, something with the Development Commission?"

"I suppose I could put in a word for him, if that's what you want."

"Oh I do."

"But maybe he'd like his old job better."

"He had to turn it in."

"Yes, but things that are changed can be changed again. I subscribe to the *Daily News* and it's a fine paper but since your father left they don't have a good fishing correspondent."

"But he wants to do something for the planet."

"Indeed. Very admirable."

"Will you help him?"

"Any way I can."

"Oh that's great." She hesitated. "Can I ask you something?"

"Certainly. Anything at all."

"Why do you wear that silly hat?"

"What's so silly about it?"

"The propellers."

"Oh." He gave each of them a flick. "I designed this hat."

"She dropped her head in embarrassment. "I'm sorry, I didn't mean—"

"No, please. It's quite all right. You see, it's kind of a test. If folks tell me it's silly, then I know they're honest. But if they tell me how interesting it is, how fashionable or something like that, then I know they're up to something."

"Does anybody really say stuff like that?"

"You'd be surprised."

"But it's sneaky," Eloise said. "They don't know it's a joke."

"I suppose you're right," Uncle Rudy said sadly. "But unfortunately, sneaky is sometimes necessary. Like you coming out here all by yourself without telling your parents. Right?"

Eloise looked down and nodded her head.

Just then the front door slammed and the whole Smith clan piled into the house, making an enormous racket.

Uncle Rudy flew Eloise home and Bill came along for the ride. The two kids sat in back and Bill told her all the things he had done and seen since the Tubs had left the neighborhood. Bill seemed as happy to see Eloise as she was to see him. In fact, just before the traveller settled down on the street in front of the Tubs' apartment building, Bill took her hand in his for just a moment. Eloise was glad it was dark and Bill could not see her face. She practically skipped up the stairs to the apartment. Things were going to be better now, she just knew it.

CHAPTER FOUR
Tourists

Then the tourists came. They came from all over the galaxy, from Aurelia to Zoopie, from the Asteroid Suspenders to the Bracelets of Saturn. They came in enormous cruise ships that darkened the sky from horizon to horizon and they came in speedy sport boats that looked like mosquitoes with fluorescent racing stripes.

The tourists came in all shapes and sizes, representatives of all the intelligent—and not so intelligent—creatures in the universe. Mostly they were humans though. They came to see Planet Wampetter because of the bigscreen advertisements put on by Mr. Smith's Development Commission. For weeks the ads saturated the airwaves. One of the galaxy's best-known actors appeared on-screen wearing a safari outfit and dark sunglasses. He removed his sunglasses and smiled.

"Are you tired of sitting home, watching the same

old shows? Tired of the same old galactic fun spots? Are you ready for an ADVENTURE? Then listen up."

The red and orange globe of Planet Wampetter appeared on the screen.

"Come journey with us to a far-off sector of the galaxy, one rarely seen by ordinary tourists." The camera zoomed over the landscape. "Fly over the barren wastes and vast mountains of this primitive wilderness. See the natives, impish and simple, their traditional ways untouched and unspoiled." There were quick shots of a noseball game and a dance contest. "Meet them, UP CLOSE AND PERSONAL. Come back with great videos! What are you waiting for? Call now, operators are standing by. Join the last great adventure of our time. Visit PLANET WAMPETTER!" Then the music came up loud, a symphony orchestra playing with a rock band.

The first time it came on Gartrude jumped up and down and yelled: "Can we go, can we go, please?"

"No, Gartrude," her mother said wearily.

"But I want to! Why can't we go?" Gartrude asked, stomping her feet and wiggling her bottom.

"Because we already live on Planet Wampetter," Eloise said.

"Oh," said Gartrude, her brow furrowed. Then her expression brightened. "No we don't! It doesn't look like that at all," she said.

Indeed it was true. Ordinary life on the planet seemed quite dull compared to the excitement of the bigscreen commercial. But the tourists only saw the commercial and so they came. Lots of them. Hordes of them. Lots of hordes of them. They crowded the streets and the stores and the restaurants and the parks. Their loud voices and loud clothes and boisterous manners filled the city with such a clamor that it seemed that there was not room for another sound or color or creature. Then even more tourists arrived.

No one minded the crowds, though, because the visitors brought money. They rented hotel rooms and travellers and bought meals and drinks. They bought cute little dolls with wobbly heads to put on traveller dashboards and bumper stickers that said: "Think Wampetter!" and "Wampetters Do It in the Mud." They bought souvenir pens and hats and banners and socks and sweat shirts and T-shirts and candy. They bought tickets for tours and special performances and they paid wampetters they met on the street to do silly things for the videos they took home to show their friends. Money seemed to fly out of their wallets and purses and pockets and for a while, wampetters everywhere felt rich.

Soon after the tourists arrived Berthe and Gartrude went to work. Berthe worked as a combination waitress, cook and dish-washer at the Ready-Before-You-Know-It Restaurant at the Spaceport. It was a very demanding job. She handled 50 tables all by herself. She took orders from the customers, entered them into her computerized order-taker, raced to the kitchen to collect the food from the computerized microwaves, then raced back to serve it. She ran back and forth because the restaurant's motto was, "Fresh

From the Microwave to Your Mouth." When the diners were finished she collected all the glasses and dishes and took them to the computerized dishwasher in the back. At the end of the day she was tired and sore. Every day she came home with a new bruise. This made Albert very upset. He thought someone was hitting her.

"You tell me who it is and I'll take care of him," Albert said fiercely, putting up his fists.

"No, dear, it's not like that. I've just fallen down a few times," Berthe said.

"Why?" asked Gartrude.

"Because she tripped. What do you think, she fell down on purpose?" Eloise said in her most sarcastic tone. Sometimes her little sister was so thick.

"Well, actually it is on purpose," Berthe said. "Falling down is part of the job."

"What?" the other Tubs asked.

"Well, the manager says that the only thing most humans know about wampetters is that we're cheerful and clumsy," Berthe explained. "So we always have to smile and every so often we're supposed to fall down and let all the plates and glasses smash on the ground. Everything's unbreakable but it makes such a noise. And the tourists love it. They laugh and clap and then they help pick things up."

"The tourists are really stupid," Gartrude said.

"I don't like that kind of talk," Berthe said sharply.

"But they are. They never listen when I give them directions. They always point their camera at me and tell me to do something funny. So I give them a butt-in-the-air."

"Gartrude!" Albert exclaimed. A butt-in-the-air is exactly what it sounds like. A traditional wampetter insult, in the old days a butt-in-the-air could start a war, or at least an argument.

"But Dad, they think it's great. They laugh and give me money," Gartrude said. "They like it."

Albert shook his head but said nothing more.

Meanwhile Eloise continued with school and Albert waited for the Development Commission to call. One night about a month after the tourists arrived, the call came. Berthe hustled the children out of the kitchen so Albert could have some privacy. She whispered to Albert. "It's Mr. Smith. It's about a job!"

Albert emerged from the kitchen ten minutes later, looking very somber.

"Well?" Berthe asked.

"Mr. Smith offered me a job." Albert paused. "They want me to put on a concert." He paused again. "A singing concert. For money."

"So you said no," Berthe said.

Albert shrugged. "He wanted me to think about it. He says I can arrange it however I want, that it would be very respectful and a chance for the rest of the galaxy to appreciate the accomplishments of wampetters. He even says we could give the money to the poor."

"But next time they have a concert they'll keep the money," Berthe observed.

"That's right. Mr. Smith says the singing will bring a lot more tourists. If I say yes then lots of other wampetters will do it too."

"The tourists are always asking us to sing," Gartrude said. "I don't, but some of the kids do and they get a lot of money even though they can hardly sing. Nothing like you Dad."

"I just remember what Grandpa Doozer said before he taught me a song," Albert said. "'Keep this special,' he said."

"What happens if you say no?" Berthe asked.

"I won't get a job. Mr. Smith says it's my only chance. He wants to know in a few days."

That Saturday, early in the morning, Eloise was snuggled deep beneath her covers in bed, when a terrible racket woke her up. Wiping sleep from her eyes she looked out the window. Down in front of their building an ancient traveller shook, rattled and roared as its engines shut down. It was the oldest traveller she had ever seen. The doors creaked open and two humans emerged: Bill and Uncle Rudy. What were they doing here, and in that old machine? Eloise wondered. But she had no time for wondering, they were coming in. She had to get dressed.

She jumped out of bed, flung off her pajamas and

leapt into her clothes, all at the same time. She had seen people do it on the bigscreen many times. But instead of ending up completely dressed the way they did on the bigscreen, she ended up in a big knot of arms and legs, sheets, pajamas, underwear, pants and shirt. In the mirror she looked like a giant orange pretzel. It took her nearly ten minutes to untangle herself and dress properly. By the time she emerged from her bedroom, Uncle Rudy and Bill were seated on the living room couch, talking with Albert. Berthe and Gartrude were already off at work.

"They want to go galumpfing!" Albert told Eloise. He looked happier than he had in weeks.

"Oooh. Can I come?" she asked.

"We wouldn't go without you," said Uncle Rudy.

"But—" began Albert.

"But what?" asked Uncle Rudy.

"The best place for galumpfing—Lake Wacawacawoo—is closed. There are signs all over: 'Keep Out. No Trespassing. Planet Wampetter Development Commission.'"

"Oh dear. The rulers again," Uncle Rudy said.

"The what?" Eloise asked.

"The rulers," Uncle Rudy said. "They're in charge of rules all over the galaxy. They go to rule school and know everything there is to know about rules: rules for chess and checkers, rules for table manners, rules for walking and driving. They know rules for everything. And when new rules are needed, they make them up. Unfortunately their favorite rule—by far—is no. It's the easiest rule of all. If you say yes then you have to say how and why and when and who and all the rest of that, but with no, that's all you need to say. Just, no, no, no."

"But the signs say keep out," Eloise observed.

"Hmmm," Uncle Rudy said. "Let's think about that. You see I was a ruler once, and I learned that as much as we need rules, we also need to test them every so often. Because if you don't test a rule, you never know if it's any good. Or what it really means. For example, these signs were put up by the Development Commission. Now if the Commission can close the area, then the Commission can open it. And since Bill and I work for the Commission, maybe we can decide that for today, for us, it should be open. That's what the rule means to me. But we can't be sure until we test it."

"Really?" asked Albert, incredulous. "We can do that?"

"Absolutely. So let's go," Uncle Rudy said. With a flick of his propellers he launched himself off the couch and headed out the door.

Uncle Rudy's traveller took a long time to warm up and then Uncle Rudy had to argue with the navigational computer about the best way to the lake. "I'm afraid this machine's a bit like me," Uncle Rudy said. "It doesn't like to take orders."

Finally the machine rose into the sky and they headed east over Foom toward the Great Plain Meadows. For an hour they flew over the tawny grasses until they reached foothills covered with dark blue bushes and short gray-green trees.

"Over there," Albert said. "That's where I like to land."

Uncle Rudy set the traveller down where Albert pointed—a meadow of blue and brownish grasses beside a swift, rocky stream.

"Where's the lake?" Bill wanted to know.

"About an hour's hike," Albert said, hoisting a knapsack to his back.

"Can't we get any closer?" he complained.

"No," said Albert.

"It's not that bad," Eloise offered. She had come with her father several times before.

Albert led them single-file across the stream and into a forest of waytall trees. Broad and dark at their roots, they tapered to pale green tops more than a hundred feet above the ground. Their branches started about halfway up and were covered with delicate whitish-yellow leaves. When a breeze came up the leaves looked like a mass of butterflies about to fly away.

Albert stopped suddenly and pointed at a tree that was marked in red about five feet off the ground. "What's this?" he asked.

"And over there," Eloise said, pointing to other trees marked the same way.

"Someone has painted the trees," Albert said.

"It's how they plan a road," Bill said brightly. "See how all the marked ones are in a straight line. They need roads for all the big equipment to build things. It's part of development. Maybe they're going to do something at the lake."

Albert shook his head.

"We don't cut down waytall trees," Eloise said. "These trees are centuries and centuries old."

Bill shrugged.

They set off again, following a narrow trail through the woods. Soon they came to a clearing where three or four enormous purple birds whirled and dove at each other, as if they were playing tag in the air.

"Yellow borangiis," Eloise told Bill.

"Purple you mean," Bill said.

"No. Yellow."

"Purple," Bill insisted.

"Yellow!" Eloise shouted.

"Purple!" Bill yelled louder.

"Bill!" Uncle Rudy shouted, louder still. "You are displaying ignorance and boorishness."

Bill stuck his hands on his hips and glared at his uncle.

"Let me explain," Albert said. "The borangiis have purple wings, but they're called yellow borangiis. That's just their name."

"It's confusing.You should change it," Bill said.

"It's not ours to change," Albert said. "The borangiis like it."

"Birds have feelings too," Eloise said.

"How do you know?" Bill asked sharply.

"Come on, we've still got a ways to go," Albert said.

They emerged from the forest a short time later into the hot bright sun and trudged up a steep hill.

Finally, sweaty and panting for breath, they reached the top. Bill and Uncle Rudy gasped. Below them, spreading as far as they could see was a lake so clear and smooth that it made a perfect mirror of the sky and its fluffy clouds. On the lake's opposite shore stood the legendary Mount Teyokk, its peak still capped with snow.

"Welcome to Lake Wacawacawoo, home of the biggest and oldest galumpfs in the galaxy," Albert announced. He led them down to the shore where, beneath a tarpaulin lay an open boat filled with ropes and paddles. On Albert's instructions they carried the boat down to the lake and clambered in. Eloise and Bill felt the cool water on their hands as they dipped their paddles in the lake.

"Look out for big ripples," Albert instructed. "That means a G's coming to the surface."

"A 'G' is a galumpf," Eloise told Bill.

"What about bait?" Bill asked. "You can't catch fish without bait. And we need hooks and rods—or maybe a harpoon."

"Galumpfs are the smartest marine creatures in the galaxy. They would never be fooled by a worm on a hook," Eloise said. "And besides, we're not trying to catch them. We're just looking for a ride."

"A ride?" asked Bill.

"First we have to let them know we're here," Albert said. "They're a little hard of hearing." He lay down his paddle and clapped his hands slowly. The others joined in. The sound echoed off the lake and the mountain. Then Albert began a loud chant:

"HIIIYAAA, HEEYAAH, HIIIYAAAH, HEEYAAH." Again the others joined in. Suddenly Albert signalled them to stop. He pointed off to the left.

"I don't see anything," Bill said.

"Oh!" exclaimed Uncle Rudy.

An enormous dark shape, like an island rising out of the lake, appeared several hundred yards away. The creature's great brow broke the surface first, followed by sad green eyes, and a long, wrinkled back. It was several times bigger than the boat.

"And over there!" yelled Bill.

"And there, a really big one!" Eloise shouted.

"Oh my goodness," said Albert. "It's Old Grouchy." He pointed out the largest of the creatures." He's nearly two hundred and fifty years old."

"What do we do now?" Uncle Rudy asked.

"Well, they're expecting some entertainment. A song, a joke, a story. They prefer something funny," Albert said.

"Me first," said Eloise. She stood in the middle of the boat, her father holding her legs steady. She cleared her throat and spoke loudly. "Why did the turkey cross the road?" She waited a moment and then shouted: "Because it was the chicken's day off!"

A deep rumbling came from the galumpfs.

Then Bill got up. "Watch this," he told them. He thought for a moment and cupped his hands around his mouth. He yelled:

Big fish, fat fish, swimming all around
Big fish, ugly fish, think you're so great.
Can't even talk, Can't even read.
Big fish, ugly fish swimming very slow
Think you're so great. Well I don't.

Eloise could not believe it. She had never heard of anyone being so rude to a galumpf. They were the most respected creatures on the planet. Of course galumpfs have been around for a long time and were not likely to pay much attention to a boy's silly poem. It was what Bill did next that caused all the trouble.

Now, everyone has a sore spot. Everyone has something that gets them really upset. Like most water creatures, galumpfs are sensitive about their appearance. They think of themselves as handsome beasts, much more attractive than fish. They hate, in fact they loathe, indeed they positively detest it when anyone makes a fish face at them.

On the trip to the lake, Albert had explained this to Bill, along with many other important facts about galumpfs, but Bill had paid no attention. So Bill had no idea what would happen when he sucked in his cheeks so his lips puckered out and made a loud sucking sound in the direction of one of the smaller galumpfs. As it turned out, Bill made a fish face to Old Grouchy's wife. Old Grouchy did not like this. Old Grouchy then showed them why he was called Old Grouchy.

The largest of the galumpfs churned into motion. He swam once around the boat and then again and again, faster and faster, closer and closer. The galumpf's swirling motion created a whirlpool that spun the boat so fast that Bill, who was still standing, flew high into the air. Eloise would never forget the way Bill screamed as he sailed out of the boat and into the great dark cavern of Old Grouchy's open mouth.

Old Grouchy clamped down on Bill as if to eat him up, but the galumpf was so old that his teeth had worn away to dull knobs. Instead Old Grouchy squeezed the boy and shook him from side to side.

"No! No!" Uncle Rudy yelled. He searched frantically for a Rescue-Pak, but they had been left in the traveller. Eloise bit her shoulder with fright.

The next thing she knew her father stood at the bow of the boat, a short club called a thumper clenched between his teeth. Albert leapt into the lake and swam furiously toward the old galumpf. He grabbed a handful of the mighty creature's loose skin and hoisted himself up its back. Old Grouchy reared up, but too late. Albert struck a mighty blow with his thumper on the mammal's thick skull, just like a legendary galumpfeteer, saving a princess from a sea monster.

Old Grouchy let out a cry of pain, a low moan like

a fog horn and Bill slipped from its mouth into the lake.

For the first time in her life, Eloise knew exactly what to do and she did exactly what she planned. She tied one end of the life preserver rope to the boat and with a great heave threw the life preserver just beyond Bill. Bill grabbed it and Eloise and Uncle Rudy reeled him in. He landed in the boat shivering, wet, and speechless.

Eloise's heart slowed with relief. Then Uncle Rudy looked out over the lake. "Oh no," he said.

Eloise looked up to see Old Grouchy's fluke disappearing into the water. The other galumpfs were gone too. So was her father. Only his blue cap lay floating on the surface.

"Where's your Dad?" Bill asked.

Eloise could not answer. Her throat felt frozen shut.

Long minutes passed. The boat rocked gently on the last ripples from the galumpfs' departure. Eloise knew her father could hold his breath for a long time, but not for as long as a galumpf.

"Oh, please, please, please," prayed Eloise. "Let him be okay." She thought awful thoughts about all the worst things that could happen and might be happening right then. Why did they ever agree to go galumpfing? Why did these humans have to come to their planet? She just wanted everything to go back to the way things used to be.

"I'm really sorry," Bill said.

Eloise could not even look at him.

When they had all just about given up hope, the water suddenly boiled around them and the lake's surface was covered with galumpfs. It was more than a school, it was a whole university of the creatures. The last to appear was Old Grouchy himself, with Albert hanging onto his neck.

"Whhoooowee!" Albert yelled.

The galumpfs responded with a chorus of whistles and booms.

"They're applauding," said an astounded Eloise. "They think it's a show."

The galumpfs circled the boat and with great ceremony unfolded their wings. Galumpf wings are not for flying, but are delicate fins covered with intricate patterns of iridescent yellow and green and purple, usually kept folded against their bodies. Usually they are shown only to other galumpfs at wedding or divorce ceremonies. Old Grouchy showed his wings last, a most impressive display of wild colors in spirals and sprays.

"Come on! Old Grouchy's in a good mood," Albert shouted. "Let's saddle up and ride."

As you can imagine, after what had happened it took a bit of persuading to get Eloise, Uncle Rudy and Bill to climb on the back of a galumpf, but eventually Albert arranged each of them on a sea horse, as they were sometimes called. Eloise settled herself in the natural depression behind her galumpf's enormous head, and held fast to the folds of thick skin around its neck.

When their riders were secure, the galumpfs set off

in formation across the lake. Eloise felt an incredible sense of speed and power in the creature beneath her. It was much more exciting than a traveller, even though the machine went faster. Soon the galumpfs began a game of tag, chasing each other while their

riders screamed with delight. When a galumpf managed to tag another with its nose, it would issue a breathy chortle that made Eloise laugh and laugh. Then they cruised the vast lake, seeing parts that even Albert had never seen before. As the sun came down low against Mount Teyokk, Albert asked the galumpfs to take them underwater. They took deep breaths, hung on tight and the galumpfs briefly showed them the wonders that lay beneath the lake's surface.

Finally they were back on shore, waving as the galumpfs slapped the water with their flukes in a farewell gesture.

As they walked back, Bill seemed different to Eloise. Where before he had paid no attention to any of the plants or animals, now he asked Eloise questions about everything he saw. He smelled the flowers and tried to touch all the plants.

"Oh, wow! Look at this thing with the yellow balls!" Bill exclaimed, rushing toward a small plant with yellow bulbs atop thick stems.

"No! Don't touch!" she yelled, as he reached out his fingers.

Bill stepped back. "Is it poisonous?"

"No. It's a puff ball plant. But if you squeeze it these tiny silver seeds come out and they'll make you blotchy all over. In the olden days when wampetters actually hunted galumpfs, they used to squeeze puff balls to make spots all over them to make them stronger or scarier or something."

"Wow," said Bill.

They started walking again.

"I'm homesick," he said.

"Is your home planet a long way away?" Eloise asked.

"I don't have one," he said.

"Everybody does. You were born somewhere. Your parents come from somewhere."

"So? The longest we've ever stayed anywhere is six months," Bill said. "I've lived on twenty different planets. I've been to twenty-three different schools.

Pretty soon we're going to have to move again and I don't want to. I want to have a birthday party where I can invite the same kids that came to my party last year."

"Why don't you pick somewhere and stay?"

"It's my Dad's job. He gets development started somewhere and then he has to leave to do it somewhere else. There are always more places to develop."

"But your family is rich. You can do what you want."

Bill shook his head. "No. All the money comes from investors. People give us money to start development but they expect us to pay them back more money later. Dad says pretty soon we'll be rich but he always says that. It's not fair."

"No, it isn't," Eloise said. "You could stay with us. I'm sure Mom and Dad wouldn't mind."

"Really?"

"Sure."

"Even though I'm not a wampetter?"

"Sure."

"Even after what I did at the lake?"

"You said you were sorry."

Bill stopped walking. "You've been a really good friend to me, Eloise. Can you keep a secret?"

"Sure."

"It's something I shouldn't tell you."

"Then don't," she said.

"I mean, I shouldn't, but I should. It's really confusing but after what happened today— Anyway, remember you asked me before about Little Jeen and his operation?"

"Is he okay?"

"Yes, he's fine. Now this is the secret. Promise not to tell anyone?"

"I promise."

"Okay." Bill took a deep breath. "Little Jeen didn't need the operation. He's been able to see for years."

"What?"

"After the first season on the show he had the operation, but they kept it a secret because they thought it might ruin the show. Everybody thought of him as the cute little blind wampetter. Then my Dad thought that making a big deal out of his getting the operation would be a good way for wampetters to learn about development."

"But he didn't need the operation."

"Right."

"Did the beautiful Hannah know that?"

"Absolutely."

"Oh, Bill. You don't know how worried we were about Little Jeen."

"But you don't even know him."

"It seemed like we did. But I guess we didn't."

"I'm sorry, Eloise."

"Thanks for telling me."

"Are we still friends?" asked Bill.

"I think so," said Eloise. She really hated lies.

Up ahead Albert and Uncle Rudy were engaged in their own conversation.

"The marks on the trees, all those red posts I saw

around the lake. What's that about?" Albert asked.

"The lake region has been laid out for a ski resort. The plan is for most of the lake to be filled in for a hotel and condominiums. The mountain will be graded for ski slopes. Most of the forest will be cleared too," Uncle Rudy said.

"But it doesn't snow except at the very top."

"At first they'll use artificial snow, made out of plastic. Then there are plans to change the weather—make the whole planet colder and less windy. It's complicated but it can be done."

"No one told us," Albert said.

"No species of plant or animal will be eliminated. My brother's planning a lakeside zoo for some of the smaller galumpfs."

"You mean put them in cages," Albert said.

"I'm sorry," Uncle Rudy replied.

"Sorry does not change anything," Albert said.

"I'm here to help you," Uncle Rudy said.

"Then tell your brother to pack up and leave. Tell them all to leave us alone."

"I can tell him that but he won't listen."

"We'll rip up the papers and give back the travellers and the money and everything," Albert said.

"It's too late. You see, once you signed the consents they invested a great deal of money and they won't leave until they make a lot more than they invested."

"How long will that take? A few months? A year?"

"Maybe fifty years. Maybe a hundred," Uncle Rudy said.

"Then we fight!" Albert shouted. "We make

thumpers and spears and swords and like the warriors of olden times we—"

"No, Albert. I saw you today and you were strong and courageous, but you would not have a chance against Association troops. If any humans are hurt by wampetters, the soldiers will come with their guns. Then wampetters will die, maybe a great many. Albert, I can only offer advice. Don't think about fighting, not that way anyway. Go back to your job. Write a story about all this."

"About the galumpfs?"

"And the mountain and the lake and the forest and what might happen to them."

Albert was silent for a long time. "Is this why you wanted to go fishing today?" he asked finally.

"Yes."

"You are a sneaky man," Albert said. "But maybe you are sneaky good."

In the traveller on the way home no one said much. They were all tired from a long day and had a great deal to consider. After the sun set over the mountains, painting the sky with streaks of purple and orange, Eloise closed her eyes. She dozed off, her head on Bill's shoulder. Soon Bill fell asleep as well.

L.J.

CHAPTER FIVE

From Bad to Worse

Because he was a star of the bigscreen, little Jeen could do just about anything he wanted. He could eat sweets for breakfast, lunch and dinner. He could stay up late at night and he never had to do his homework.

At least once a day little Jeen did something to remind everyone he was a star. If he did not get what he wanted as fast as he wanted, or if he was not getting enough attention, or if he just felt ornery, he threw a temper tantrum. He screamed and bounced off the walls until folks came running with his favorite candy and offered to read him stories and give him presents and be his best friend forever. When he finally calmed down someone would always tell him what a wonderful actor he was and how it was good for you to scream every so often.

There were some bad things about being a star though. Little Jeen knew that the same folks who smiled at him sweetly when he entered the room, said nasty things about him when he left. He almost never got to see his parents or brothers and sisters because they lived off in the country, far from the studio where they shot *A Family Wampetter*. But the worst part of being a star was that no one ever told him when he did something wrong. As a result, he developed some bad habits, like spying on people.

When he did not have to be on the set, little Jeen loved to sneak around and listen in on other folks' conversations, and watch what they did when they thought they were alone. Most of all he liked to spy on the beautiful Hannah. Little Jeen did not like Hannah. She was an even bigger star than he and so she could be mean to him if she wanted to, and she often did. Half the time she screamed at him for being a little brat and the other half she gave him fake smiles and kisses, which was even worse.

On the morning before they were to shoot the most important episode of the year, the one where he took off his bandages from the operation and saw for the first time, little Jeen arrived at the set early. When he saw Hannah walk down the hallway to her dressing room, little Jeen knew just what to do. After she entered her dressing room, he ducked into the storage closet next door and put his ear to the wall. He heard a man speaking to Hannah.

"Just think, Planet Wampetter will be the first planet in the whole galaxy devoted totally to entertainment, the first one controlled by a single company." Little Jeen recognized the voice of Mr. Smith. "But we have to make sure the wampetters sign their work papers."

"Just tell them to do it," Hannah said. "They're so stupid they'd sign toilet paper if you told them to."

"Please, Hannah. Someone might hear you. They trust you. That's why we'd like you to do one last announcement on the show. Tell the wampetters that it'll make them happy beyond their wildest dreams."

Hannah laughed, a wild, harsh sound. "I guess I won't tell them the truth, then."

"No. They wouldn't understand anyway."

"And what will you do for me?" Hannah asked.

"Well, you're an investor so you'll be making money for yourself. And there's one other thing. After the next phase we'll hold elections. We thought you might like to be the first President of Theme Planet Wampetter. It would be quite an honor.

"Wow," said Hannah.

Little Jeen listened hard while Mr. Smith explained what would happen in the next phase of development. The more he heard the worse little Jeen felt. It was awful. He knew he had to tell someone. But who? He had no real friends. Then he thought of Bill, Mr. Smith's son. They had done some things together. He seemed like a good kid. But could little Jeen trust him?

Taking Uncle Rudy's advice, Albert returned to his job at the paper to write about the development plans for Lake Wacawacawoo. He found out that the Development Commission had put big ads about the project in magazines and on the bigscreen on other planets, just nothing on Planet Wampetter. Albert's story appeared on the front page of the *Daily News* under the headline: "LAKE WACAWACAWOO TO BE DESTROYED; GALUMPFS TO BE CAGED." The story caused a great sensation. Wampetters everywhere were furious. Many gathered outside the Development Commission office and stuck thumbs in their ears at talkers who went in and out. This was a terrible insult but the talkers paid no attention.

The following day Mr. Smith came by to see Albert.

"I'm very disappointed in you," Mr. Smith said,

waving the newspaper in front of him. "After all we've done for you. I thought we were friends."

"You never told us about the lake."

"You never asked. Look, to make an omelette you need to break some eggs. In development you can't worry about every little tree and fish. Now what you need to do is write a story saying that this was all a misunderstanding."

"You're not going to make the ski resort?" Albert asked.

"Of course we are. We just don't want anyone upset about it. No one'll mind once it's built."

Albert solemnly shook his head.

Mr. Smith's lips quivered with anger. "I've already bought your paper. If you don't do as I say you'll lose your job and so will all your friends."

Albert shook his head again.

"You've done a lot of shopping You owe more than two thousand parbils for all the items you bought on credit. How are you going to pay it back?" Mr. Smith demanded.

"We'll return everything."

"The stores won't take it back. It's too late," Mr. Smith said.

"We'll sell the traveller you gave us."

"Too late again. I'm taking that back."

"But you can't, it was a gift."

"Only for as long as we were friends. I thought that would be forever. The papers for the traveller are still in my name. Do you really think I'd give away a top-of-the-line machine for nothing?" Mr. Smith tried a smile. "Albert. Don't make things hard for you or your family."

"Leave my family out of it!" Albert yelled.

"Berthe and Gartrude will lose their jobs too," Mr. Smith promised.

"I won't do it," Albert insisted.

"You'll be very sorry," Mr. Smith said.

Mr. Smith did everything he said he would. Albert and most of his friends were fired from the paper. A talker from the Development Commission took the traveller away, Berthe and Gartrude lost their jobs and the stores demanded payment for all the things Albert bought and would not take them back. He had two weeks to come up with the money or he would have to go to another planet to work.

When the Tubs sat down to watch the season finale of *A Family Wampetter,* even Gartrude was silent and glum. They all wondered what would happen to Albert.

On the show little Jeen returned to Planet Wampetter after his operation, his eyes still bandaged. Finally little Jeen could wait no longer. He snuck into the bathroom and pulled off the bandages himself. The first thing he saw was his own face in the mirror. He jumped up and fell down. He leapt up again.

"I can see! I can see! For the first time in my life I can see!" he shouted.

Then, you had to be looking for it, but to wampetter's eyes the signal he gave was quite clear. Little Jeen wiggled one ear. For wampetters, wiggling both ears is a sign of joy, but wiggling one ear signals a trick. It means the wampetter is not telling the truth. It's just like human children who cross their fingers or politicians who make promises to voters.

"See, I told you!" Gartrude yelled, pointing at the screen. "It's all a fake. He wasn't blind at all."

The theme song for the show came on. Berthe switched off the bigscreen.

"How did you know?" Eloise asked Gartrude, for Eloise had not repeated Bill's story to anyone.

"Everyone knew," Gartrude said.

"Well I didn't," Albert said. "You might have told me, it would have been a good story for the paper. If I still had a job. But how do you know it's true?"

"It is," Eloise said.

"How do you know?" Berthe asked Eloise.

"I can't say."

"Bill told you, right?" Gartrude demanded.

"I can't say," Eloise repeated.

Berthe sat down heavily. "Oh dear. And I thought it was all talk. Oh, Albert. I never thought they'd send you away. But if they've been lying all this time about little Jeen—" her voice trailed off.

"I know," Albert said.

A few moments later the door bell rang. For a moment no one moved. What if they were coming to take Albert away? The bell rang again.

"Coming," said Albert.

The family clustered behind him as he opened the door. Eloise and Gartrude screamed. Standing in the doorway was little Jeen himself, along with Bill and Uncle Rudy. Eloise and Gartrude screamed and stomped and bounced off the floor. The most famous wampetter of all was at their house!

When the girls finally calmed down, Bill explained why they had come. "Little Jeen told me about something that he heard that sounded very bad, so I decided to check on it. These are the plans for the next phase of development. We have to do something."

Bill laid the papers on the dining room table and they huddled around to read them.

"No!" shouted Berthe.

"This can't be right," Albert said.

"It's not fair," Eloise exclaimed.

"I don't understand!" yelled Gartrude, who could not read.

"It says that the Development Commission is going to send most wampetters away from Planet Wampetter because they're not needed here," Bill explained. "You heard the announcement Hannah made before the show? That's why they need everyone to get work papers. So they can figure out who will stay and who will go."

"Not me!" yelled Gartrude.

"Don't worry, dear. They won't send children," Berthe said.

"But they will when we grow up," Eloise said.

"The beautiful Hannah won't let them," Gartrude said.

"She hates wampetters," Little Jeen replied.

The Tubs looked at little Jeen in astonishment and horror.

"It's true," Bill said. "She's been over to our house.

She thinks wampetters are lazy good-for-nothings who can't be trusted. She's not a nice person. Not like on the show at all. We came over because we have to do something."

Albert shook his head. "I've tried. And because of that they're sending me away."

"They can't!" Eloise shouted.

"Time soothes all hurts," Albert said, repeating an ancient wampetter saying.

"But your tummy can't grow if you don't feed your mouth," Berthe responded, repeating another such saying.

"We have to do something," Eloise insisted.

"But what?" Berthe asked.

And so they sat down to talk.

The idea started with Gartrude. "You can't make humans do anything. They just do what they want."

"Exactly!" said Uncle Rudy.

"Maybe we can pay them lots of money to go away," Eloise. "They'd like that."

"But we don't have lots of money," Albert said.

"Or we can give them something they don't want," Berthe said. "That they have to keep if—I don't know."

"Something really yucky that'll make them listen," Gartrude said.

"Ooooh," they all said. There were so many possibilities. They talked and argued and paced around the room and made lists and charts and argued some more. Slowly a plan took shape.

For the next week the Tubs worked from the

moment the sun peeked through the windows in the morning until late at night, when they fell into bed exhausted. The plan was all they thought about and all they talked about.

The family took a day-long expedition to Lake Wacawacawoo. They harvested the critical ingredients for their concoction in the marshes and fields surrounding the lake, filling huge bags which they lugged back to the traveller they had borrowed from Uncle Rudy. The next day they awoke sore and tired, but that did not stop them. No one even complained.

Berthe manufactured the necessary equipment. Soon the living room was strewn with bicycle pumps and hoses and bottles of hair spray. At the other end of the room Albert worked on costumes. He was quite a skilled sewer and not bad at papier mache.

Little Jeen called every few hours to see how things were going and urge them to hurry. He said the beautiful Hannah was leaving the planet in a few days for a tour of the galaxy and they had to act before then. Bill stopped by at least once a day to tell them what he had learned about Commission plans.

None of them had done anything like this before so there were some problems. Bill said that because the plan required exact timing, each of them should wear two watches, in case one broke during the expedition. They borrowed some extra watches from friends so that they all had two, and then carefully set the watches to the same time. The only difficulty was that some of the watches ran a bit slower than others and then they had to remember which was the right time and which the wrong. Eloise forgot if it was the watch on her right arm that was slow—or was it fast? Or maybe the watch on the right arm was right, and on the left arm was wrong. She couldn't figure it out, so she borrowed a third watch from a neighbor downstairs and set it in between the other two. When Bill saw this he yelled at her that she was messing up everything because now she had no idea what the right time was. In the end, they decided each of them would only wear one watch and would check them right before they left.

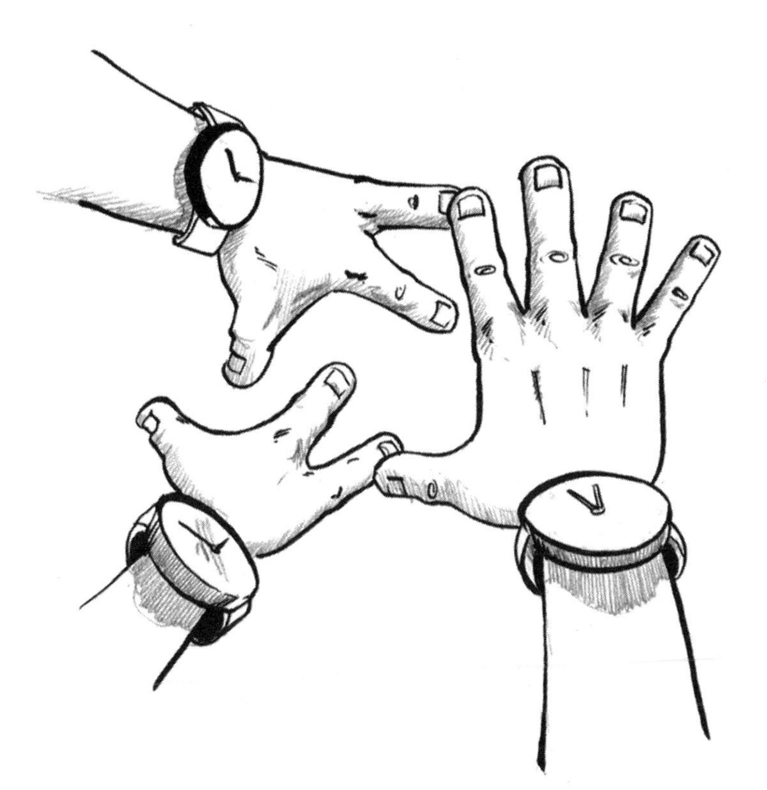

The next problem was secrecy. Bill said they needed a secret code for messages and a password for entering the apartment. The Tubs, especially Eloise and Gartrude, thought these were great ideas. It was just like a show on the bigscreen!

The next morning Bill knocked on the door to the apartment.

"Who's there?" Gartrude asked.

"Noseball," he replied.

Noseball was the password Bill had chosen for the day, except that Gartrude and Eloise didn't like it, so they changed the password to Stupidhead, one of their favorite words, especially because their parents didn't like them to say it. Unfortunately they never told Bill of the change. That wouldn't have been so bad but the girls had also decided that, to be really tricky, they would speak in code. They decided to use their favorite code. This was a code where 'no' means 'yes' and 'yes' means 'no.' They did not tell Bill about this either.

"Hey, come on, let me in," Bill said.

"What's the password?" Eloise asked.

"Noseball!" Bill yelled.

"That's right!" Gartrude yelled—of course meaning the opposite.

"So let me in. Come on, it's me, Bill. Please?"

"Okay," said Eloise—of course meaning not okay.

This went on for a while, Bill asking to be let in and the girls saying 'yes' when they meant 'no.' As you can imagine, Bill got pretty mad.

"I hate this!" he yelled. Then he had an idea. "Did

you change the password?" he demanded.

"Yes—I mean no," Gartrude said.

That gave Bill another clue. "Does 'no' mean 'yes'?"

"No," said Eloise laughing, for of course she meant 'yes.'

"You can't change the password without telling anyone," Bill said.

"But you said to keep it a secret," Gartrude said.

"Not from me."

"You said not to tell anyone," Eloise insisted.

Bill screamed with frustration. "Just tell me the new password!"

"It's a secret," Gartrude said.

Fortunately, Albert just then came home from the market and let Bill in. After that they decided to do without passwords and codes.

Meanwhile, every night there were stories on the news about big changes on the planet. There were terrible pictures from the spaceport of wampetter families shouting and wailing because a relative was being sent to another planet, their punishment for breaking Development Commission rules. The news showed other pictures of long lines of wampetters waiting for their work papers. Soon, the reporter said, everyone would have their papers and the next phase of development would begin. Time was growing short.

The night before the expedition the Tubs had just sat down to dinner when they heard a great thud on the front door.

"Open up, police!" a deep voice yelled.

Berthe checked the room to make sure that everything was hidden and then nodded to Albert. Albert opened the door. Two enormous police officers

in purple uniforms with huge guns strapped to their chests stood there.

"Albert R. Tub?" said the larger of the two. "I hereby issue you this Notice to Expel. You have three days to report to the spaceport for mandatory relocation for failure to pay your bills. Have a good night and a better tomorrow." He thrust a paper into Albert's hands and then the two of them marched away.

The Tubs clustered around Albert, trying to read the paper.

"Look, you have a choice," Berthe said. "You can go to the Yaww system to work on asteroid clearance, or to Pancreez to work in a toothpaste factory. Or you can go to Mmneew and do recycling. Maybe that's not too bad."

"But Mom," said Eloise. "Erasing pencil marks from papers is so boring."

"It's only for a year," Albert said softly.

"A year!" Berthe shrieked.

"Maybe I should do the concert," Albert said. "What if our plan doesn't work? What if we get caught?"

No one said anything for a long time.

"We have to do it," Eloise said finally.

"But I'm scared," said Gartrude.

"The only really scary thing is being scared," replied Eloise, repeating an old wampetter saying. "You can't do the concert Dad, it's wrong. And we won't let them take you."

"That's right," Gartrude said.

"Absolutely," Berthe added.

"We're all in this together," said Eloise.

Albert smiled. His eyes sparkled. "Maybe you're right. Maybe we should give it the old wampetter try." He paused a moment. "Okay. We'll do it."

By the following night everything was ready. Uncle Rudy's traveller was loaded with the costumes and the spraying equipment. They were about to leave when little Jeen appeared at the door.

"What are you doing here?" Eloise demanded. They were supposed to meet him at Hannah's house.

"I can't do it!" he said, his voice cracking. "I have my career to consider. It's okay for you guys, you have nothing to lose. I just can't help any more."

"But how do I know where to go? You said it was a big house," Eloise said.

"Yeah, it's huge. But you just go upstairs. Then it's down the hallway to the right, then take a left and another left. Or is it left down the hallway? I'm not sure. But you'll figure it out." And with that little Jeen disappeared.

"Everyone's chickening out," Gartrude said.

"Just little Jeen," Eloise said. "Bill said he'll leave the back door open for us—for me."

"Can you manage everything?" Berthe asked.

"Sure," said Eloise, but actually she wasn't so sure.

Hannah's house sat atop a big hill in the most expensive part of Foom. A fence surrounded the whole property. On it were posted big signs saying, "No Trespassing," and, "If You're Not Invited, Go Home." There was even a sign that said: "Wampetters

Will Be Shot on Sight." A searchlight atop the house swept slowly across the lawn around the house, looking for any intruders. Little Jeen said that Hannah had guards with guns.

"I'm really scared," said Gartrude as she looked up at the house from behind the fence.

"You'll be okay," Eloise said. She was even less sure than before.

Albert and Berthe boosted them over the wall, then handed over the equipment and costumes.

"Good luck," said Berthe.

"We'll be here waiting," said Albert.

Eloise and Gartrude put on their costumes. Just like Surprise Day, they dressed as natural objects. Gartrude was a brindlebush and Eloise was a waytall tree. Surprise Day was named after an ancient wampetter battle won by a small tribe which snuck up on a much larger force during the night by dressing as trees and bushes and creeping across a field so quietly and slowly that when the sun came up the next morning, all the attackers had to do was jump up and say, "Surprise" and their enemies surrendered. Gartrude and Eloise hoped that the costumes would let them cross the lawn to the house without being noticed.

Eloise felt her knees shake as she watched the searchlight cross the lawn.

"Okay, when the light goes by we run as far as we can, then stop when the light comes back," Eloise said.

"I'm not a stupidhead," Gartrude complained. "I know the plan."

NO
TRESPASS

"Then go!" Eloise yelled.

They ran toward the house as fast as their short legs could go. If anyone had been watching closely they would have been astonished to see a small waytall tree and a large brindlebush running across the lawn. Fortunately for the girls no one was watching closely. There was a big party at the house that night, and everyone inside was having much too good a time to pay much attention to anything outside. When the searchlight swept over them they crouched down and made like vegetation.

Finally the girls reached the back door.

"Okay, I'll see you in a few minutes," Eloise said. The plan was for Gartrude to wait outside and keep a lookout. If she saw anything she was to cry like a yellow borangii.

"I don't want to," Gartrude said.

"Why not?" Eloise asked.

"Because I have to go potty," Gartrude said.

"We asked you before we left the house," Eloise said.

"I didn't need to go then. Now I do." She hopped from one foot to the other.

"Then go on the ground. No one can see you under that bush anyway."

"That's gross," Gartrude complained.

"Too bad," said Eloise. She reached for the back door knob and twisted. It opened. Eloise felt a great relief as she stepped inside. Everything was going to be okay. In her haste to enter the house, though, Eloise had forgotten that she was still wearing her waytall tree costume. Forgetting to duck, she jammed her top branches against the ceiling and wedged the trunk against the floor. She pulled and poked and wriggled and pushed but she could not free herself. From nearby came the sounds of a human party. Any minute someone would come and discover her and the whole family would all be sent away from the planet forever.

"Gartrude—help!" Eloise whispered.

"What did you say?" Gartrude asked loudly.

"Help me, I'm stuck!"

"What do you want me to do?"

"Just do something!"

"Okay, okay."

Gartrude took off her costume. She pulled on her sister, then pushed, but Eloise stayed stuck.

"Hold on. I'll do a flying butt-in-the-air."

"No—" said Eloise. But it was too late.

Gartrude took a long running start. She ran as fast as she could and then at the last second she jumped, turned in the air and smacked straight into Eloise with her butt. With a great crashing sound the two burst through the doorway and landed in the back hallway.

Eloise looked at her sister.

"You wanted help," Gartrude said.

"Hurry up and get out of here before someone comes," Eloise said. "I'll be back as fast as I can."

"Good luck," said Gartrude.

Then Eloise was alone. She climbed out of her costume and shoved what was left of it into a nearby closet. From the other end of the house she heard music, laughter, shouting and singing. The scent of fresh-cooked food hung in the air. For just a moment Eloise was tempted to join the party. Instead she hurried upstairs, her equipment clanging on the bannister.

At the top of the stairs she looked around. Which way?

It was an enormous house with long wide hallways and high ceilings. The floors were of rare woods and the walls were covered with grand paintings. All around were antiques, including chairs that looked so old and delicate that they might collapse if you just sneezed near them. Eloise could not remember any of little Jeen's directions, so she tried every door on the hallway. She found a study and a music room and a toy room and an ordinary bedroom and then, as soon as she opened the door, she knew she had found the beautiful Hannah's bedroom.

It was huge, bigger than the entire Tub family apartment. Everywhere there were pictures Hannah. There were little pictures and big posters of Hannah: Hannah in various bigscreen roles, Hannah with other beautiful people and very important people, with kings and queens and presidents and prime ministers.

As Eloise stepped into the room she saw something that made her heart stop. On the other side of the room she saw a wampetter, carrying all kinds of strange things, staring straight at her.

"Oh!" Eloise said with a start. Then she realized she was looking at herself in a mirror. There were lots of mirrors.

Where's the bathroom? Eloise wondered. Again she tried all the doors. She found rooms full of clothes—one full of dresses and another of coats and a third of shoes. Finally she came to the bathroom. It was about the size of their living room at home. Eloise opened all the cabinets and took the tops off the powders and lotions and creams and every other kind of beauty aid you could imagine—and a lot you never could. She worked feverishly. What if someone came in! She would be doomed. Her family would be doomed. Her planet would be doomed. She could not think about it.

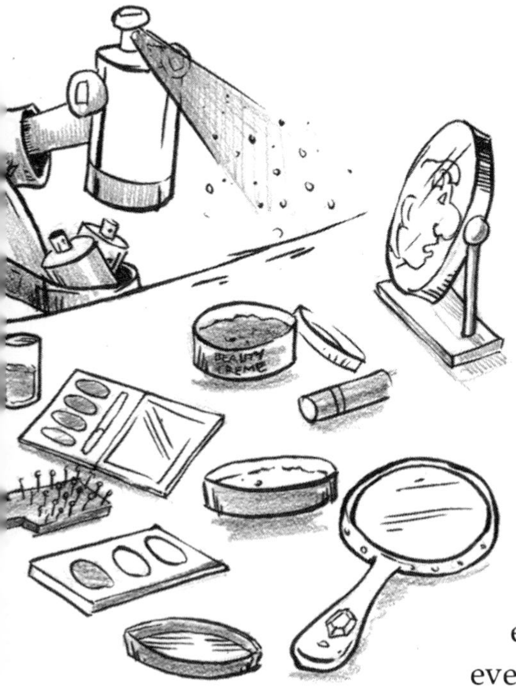

She pumped up the pressure on her sprayer, just like her mother had shown her, and carefully squeezed the trigger. A stream of infinitesimal bits glittered in the light for a moment, then disappeared. She sprayed everywhere.

The rest happened as if in a blur. She screwed the tops back on everything, rearranged everything as it had been before and ran out of the room and down the stairs and out the back door.

"Gartrude?" Eloise called softly. There was no answer. Near the house were several bushes but none of them looked like her sister. "It's me, Eloise," she said a bit louder. Still there was no reply. Eloise groaned. This was no time for one of Gartrude's little games. Eloise stamped her foot.

"Ow! You stepped on me!" Gartrude complained,

and a bush lifted up to reveal two wampetter legs.

"Well you could have said something," Eloise complained.

"I was asleep. It's past my bedtime."

"Well come on, let's go home," Eloise said.

They ran across the lawn the same way they had come, stopping each time the searchlight came by, but this time Eloise hid behind Gartrude's bush. They practically flew over the fence and into the arms of their waiting parents.

"We did it! We did it!" Gartrude yelled.

Eloise was annoyed because Gartrude had not been much help and here she was trying to take all the credit. Eloise felt like slugging her, but she was so relieved she burst into tears instead. Albert and Berthe hustled them both into the traveller and soon they were on their way home.

"Whatever happens, I want you girls to know, I'm terribly proud of you," Berthe said.

"We both are," Albert added.

But the question was, What would happen next?

CHAPTER SIX

The Great Panic

The sun filtered through the gauzy curtains as if through a cloud. The songbirds on the balcony outside chirped softly. Hannah stirred in her big bed and thought about the glorious times that lay ahead. Tomorrow she would leave for a grand tour of the galaxy. Everywhere she went people would treat her like a queen. They would tell her how beautiful she was and what a wonderful actress and how generous and wise she had been in helping the wampetters. They would all ask about her future plans. She would only say that it would be something very important. In a few weeks Mr. Smith would nominate her for president and of course all the wampetters would vote for her. In a month she would be the president of a whole planet. And then who knows? She might end up as the Grand High Chief Master of the whole Association, the leader of the whole galaxy. Why not? She was the beautiful Hannah.

She yawned and stretched and snapped her fingers. In the bathroom the bath automatically filled with water at the perfect temperature. Fresh coffee brewed in her coffee maker. String music flowed from hidden speakers. She slipped her feet into her slippers. She stood up and smiled at herself in the mirror. Then she screamed.

Her scream was heard for miles: a horrible, piercing cry, like an animal in pain, like a thousand bedsheets ripped apart. She screamed and clutched her face and pulled at her hair because overnight her skin had turned to bright orange with big black spots.

Hannah dashed to the bathroom and scrubbed her face and neck and shoulders—but it did not come off. She collapsed to the floor, sobbing. What had happened?

Of course, what had happened was that Eloise had sprayed Hannah's dressing room and cosmetics with the seeds of many puff ball plants. The effect on her skin would disappear after a few weeks and was entirely harmless, but Hannah did not know that, and neither did any of the other humans who experienced the same thing.

That same morning panic also struck the Smith family. It started it when Z came down for breakfast.

"Z, I want you to go straight upstairs and take off whatever it is you put on your face," Mrs. Smith said. "It's not funny."

"What are you talking about Mom?" Z asked. "And why do you look like a wampetter with spots?"

"Don't talk back to me," Mrs. Smith said sharply. But she nearly fainted after looking in the bathroom mirror. She did look like a wampetter with spots.

It turned out that the whole Smith family woke up

looking like wampetters with spots because Bill had sprayed the house the night before, using a sprayer Berthe had made.

"We must not panic. We must stay calm," Mr. Smith said. "It is in times like this that we see what we are made of."

"We're made of orange juice and black spots," Y said, giggling.

"Oh, no," Mr. Smith said, looking at his hands. "I have it too." Mr. Smith knew that in the far-off parts of the galaxy there were strange and deadly diseases so unknown that they did not even have names. He was too young to die—wasn't he?

Meanwhile the Tubs kept busy. The morning after the adventure at Hannah's house, Berthe, Gartrude and Eloise set off around the city with bags of puff balls to leave for the tourists. They left seed pods with holes poked in them everywhere that tourists gathered—in restaurants and hotels and souvenir shops and the parks.

Albert stayed home and handled the phone calls.

Little Jeen called around noon. "It's working," he whispered. "Every human doctor in the sector has been called to Hannah's house. She's planning to take the shuttle to Planet Xygee for special treatment tonight."

"Thanks," said Albert.

"I'm sorry I couldn't make it last night—"

"It's okay," said Albert.

"It's because of my fans. All the little wampetters

look up to me. If I get in trouble they get confused and—"

"We managed without you," Albert said.

"But I set it up. It was all my idea," Little Jeen insisted.

"I have to go," Albert said, and hung up the phone. He did not have much patience with celebrities.

Albert called a few of his reporter friends who worked on other planets. He told them he had a hot tip that Hannah was coming in on the evening shuttle to Xygee and would have something important to say. He said it was going to be BIG news. Within a few hours reporters all over the galaxy were frantic with excitement. They did not know what was happening but they were sure that it involved the beautiful Hannah and it was BIG!

That night the Tubs ate dinner early and then sat down in front of the bigscreen to watch the intergalactic news.

The announcer came on looking excited. "We have big news, sensational news, incredible news about one of the biggest, most sensational, incredible celebrities in the galaxy. For the story, let's go to Johnny Handsome, LIVE on Planet Xygee."

A strikingly handsome journalist came on the screen holding a big microphone with a picture of an ear on it up to his mouth. He spoke with great intensity. "I'm standing here, LIVE, at the spaceport on Xygee where a few hours ago we witnessed an extraordinary scene with one of the biggest bigscreen stars in the galaxy. We don't want to start any panic, but it appears that the beautiful Hannah has contracted a serious skin condition while on Planet Wampetter. This is what happened when Hannah got off the ship."

The screen showed a crowd of reporters and cameras pointed at a large spaceship which passengers were leaving. A hooded figure tried to run out, but was surrounded by reporters. The hood fell off—it was Hannah. She looked a little different than she usually did on the bigscreen. Her face looked like a rotten orange.

"Leave me alone!" she cried.

The reporters shouted questions: "What's wrong with your face? How long have you had the condition? Is it contagious? When will you be going back to Planet Wampetter? Do you have anything to say to your fans?"

Hannah exploded. "Leave me alone, you creeps! I'm never going back to Planet Wampetter, that dirty, filthy, disgusting place where they have grotesque diseases and squat little creatures that whine and do nothing all day long. I hate the place and I hate wampetters and they should all be taken out and shot!" Then Hannah pushed her way through the crowd and into a waiting limousine.

The reporter appeared on screen again. "An extraordinary scene, like nothing else this reporter has ever earwitnessed. Apparently Hannah has been admitted to the Holy Technology Hospital of Xygee and is now resting comfortably. For background on her medical condition, here is our medical expert on wampetter diseases, Dr. Mindy Plump."

Dr. Mindy, as she was known, was a famous wampetter doctor and author. Her works included a diet book, *How to Avoid Undereating*, and a book on teenage sex called, *Don't Rub Noses With Strangers You Don't Know.* She had a kindly face and manner but no one knew if she was a very good doctor.

"Dr. Mindy, have you ever seen anything like the beautiful Hannah's condition before?" the reporter asked.

"Never on a human. But we've seen it here on the planet quite a lot. You should realize that it's not malevolent. It's purely cosmetic."

"What does that mean?"

"It means that it makes you look different, but it won't hurt you."

"How long does it last?"

"Good question. It's important the public doesn't panic, because even though the condition does last for a—"

The rest of her answer was cut off by the news announcer who said: "Thanks Johnny, reporting LIVE from Planet Xygee. We'll have updates on the hour to let you know the latest on the beautiful Hannah."

"I feel sorry for her," Gartrude said as Albert switched off the set.

"Didn't you hear what she said about us and our planet?" Eloise asked.

"Yes, but she looked so ugly. And it's your fault," Gartrude said accusingly.

"No," said Albert. "Don't blame your sister. We all

did this. I'm sorry that we had to, but we did. And she'll be fine in a while."

"Do you think she really hates us?" Eloise asked. "What did we ever do to her? We loved her show and Little Jeen and everything."

"I don't think she likes anyone very much," Berthe said. "And especially creatures who aren't as beautiful as she."

"Maybe now she'll realize that's stupid," said Eloise.

"We can always hope," said Berthe. "But right now it's time for bed. We all need a good night's sleep."

The girls headed to bed without complaint, for they were very tired.

"Do you think it's going to work?" Eloise asked her father when he came in to kiss her good night.

"It's too soon to tell," Albert said. "We have a lot more work to do. But we've made a good start. And I'm very very proud of you."

Her father's words made her feel warm inside as she snuggled down for a long sleep.

When she woke up the next morning and looked out the window, the city looked different to Eloise. She wondered what it was. The sun was out and wampetters scurried along the sidewalks. A street vendor was selling fresh fruit in front of the building. Everything looked normal. Except there were no tourists.

When the Tubs took a walk later they saw that the restaurants and the souvenir shops were empty. At the spaceport, though, long lines of tourists stretched into the street. Announcements came over a loud speaker:

"Please, do not push. There are ships for everyone. Please do not panic. The skin condition will not harm your health and we believe it will wear off soon. Please, no pushing in line."

As the Tubs came around a corner, they nearly bumped into a family of tourists.

"Aaaaahh!" yelled the mother in the group. "Get away—wampetters."

The humans dashed across the street.

Albert laughed."They can't leave fast enough," he said.

Indeed, the tourists left even faster than they had come. Hordes of them left the first day after the news broke and lots of hordes on the day after that. Most were not affected by the puff balls, but it only took a few people with orange skin and spots for the rest to panic. Within three days the only humans left on the planet were people who worked for the Commission.

The Tubs did not hear from Bill or Uncle Rudy until Saturday morning, when Uncle Rudy called and invited them over for Sunday lunch.

The Tubs rode out in their old traveller, after Albert had spent the morning doing necessary repairs. The traveller was as slow and bumpy, cramped and uncomfortable as they remembered. But it was theirs and no one could take it away.

It was Change Season again and new grasses covered the hills of their old neighborhood. Insects and birds made a cheerful noise. A patch of brilliant green ooflowers bloomed in front of the Smiths' house.

Uncle Rudy greeted them at the door. "Come on,

SPACEPORT
GATES 1-1000

TICKET
PLANET
WAMPETTER

friends. Don't worry about my brother, he's just a little upset."

Mr. Smith was in the kitchen, yelling. "I'm ruined! Totally ruined. All the tourists have left and no one's coming back. The hotels are empty, the restaurants are empty and our investors are screaming. They want to know why we never told them about this disease. And I tell them, you can't know everything—and besides, it's harmless. But everyone just panics. It's a disaster!"

His wife touched his shoulder gently. "Don't worry, dear. We'll manage," she said. Mrs. Smith's face was covered with a thick white goo, like cream cheese. It made her look very strange.

"Maybe this isn't a good place for development," Bill suggested.

"There's no such thing!" Mr. Smith roared.

"Hi," said Albert.

"Hi yourself," Mr. Smith barked. "You know what happened here this week? A conspiracy. Somebody planned this whole thing. I've already called the Federal Cabinet of Investigation and they're going to look into it." He turned to Eloise. "Do you know who they are?" he asked.

"No," she whispered.

"They're humans who never smile and always wear suits and they always find out EVERYTHING and they love putting creatures in jail for a long time for breaking the rules. What do you think about that?"

Eloise ran to her mother and clutched her skirt. Now they were really in trouble.

"Oh, Richard. Don't make a federal case out of it,"

Mrs. Smith said. "You're scaring our friends. Your only mistake was relying on Hannah. She's a mean person."

"That wouldn't have mattered if she didn't panic. I don't suppose you'd be willing to do that concert for us," he asked Albert.

"No. I'm truly sorry but I cannot."

"Doesn't really matter. No one would come anyway."

"So what are you going to do?" Albert asked.

"We'll wait till the panic dies down. In a year or two people will have forgotten all about it. They're already coming back to the resorts on Planet Caull and it's only been two years since the nuclear explosion and toxic waste spill. In the meantime you wampetters will have to pay for the new buildings and roads and everything else the Commission has done for your planet."

"How much is that?" Albert asked.

"If every wampetter works for us for the next twenty years, that'll just about pay it off."

"But we never asked for anything," Berthe protested.

"What do you think that consent was for? Improving the planet. And somebody has to pay, the investors insist on that."

"But it's not fair, you didn't tell us about any of this," Eloise said sharply.

"We answered all questions," Mr. Smith said. "It's not our fault you didn't ask the right ones. We were always completely honest."

"That's not true!" Eloise exclaimed.

"Really. I don't have time for this," Mr. Smith said.

"Better hear it now than in a courtroom later," Uncle Rudy said.

"Courtroom?" Albert and Berthe asked, hands to their mouths. Wampetters hardly ever went to court and found the whole idea scary.

"Certainly," Uncle Rudy said. "If anyone connected with the Development Commission lied to you about development, you wouldn't have to pay anything. In fact, if they lied and you suffered as a result, you could sue the Commission for a great deal of money."

"Really?" said Albert. "We could?"

"Now, now, now, let's not get carried away," Mr. Smith said. He turned to Eloise. "My dear sweet child. What do you think we weren't totally honest about?"

"About how Hannah loved us and loved the planet," Eloise said.

"She did," Mr. Smith replied. "What she said the other day—she was just upset about her face. That wasn't the real Hannah at all."

"That's not—" Bill began.

"Bill—" said Mrs. Smith warningly. Bill shut his mouth.

"And you lied about Little Jeen needing an operation. He wasn't blind at all," Eloise said.

"Who told you that?" Mr. Smith demanded.

"We know for a fact that Little Jeen did not need that operation," Berthe said. "He told us."

"Brother, that's serious," Uncle Rudy told Mr. Smith. "You used Little Jeen's operation to get the Consents. This sounds like fraud."

"No, no, no, no, no!" exclaimed Mr. Smith. "Maybe there was some mistake about the operation but we never lied. I certainly had absolutely no idea. Little Jeen looked blind to me. I guess he was a better actor than anyone thought." Mr. Smith smiled, hoping that everyone would take it as a joke, but no one did.

"When he came to the house we played ball," Bill said.

"Well, maybe he could see big things from far away, but—"

"Dear—don't you remember how he read the

children a story?" Mrs. Smith asked.

"Whose side are you on?" Mr. Smith screamed. "Okay, I admit we stretched the truth a little. But Little Jeen was born blind and then he had an operation. We just changed the dates a little. What's the big deal? Nobody was hurt."

"My dad lost his job and wampetters were sent away and you were going to hurt the galumpfs and the trees and everything!" Eloise shouted.

"Now there's no need to get emotional," Mr. Smith said, patting Eloise on the head. "I know how you wampetters get emotional."

"Does that mean that what they did was against the rules?" Berthe asked Uncle Rudy.

"Yes."

"And if somebody does something bad to you against the rules, then—"

"Then you can go to court and get them to pay you a lot of money to make up for the bad thing they've done," Uncle Rudy said.

"A lot of money?" asked Gartrude.

"In this case, since they lied to a whole planet, it would be a great deal of money," Uncle Rudy replied.

"Oh, no!" Mr. Smith exclaimed. "Now I'm totally utterly completely ruined."

Uncle Rudy leaned over and whispered to his brother. "Perhaps you can negotiate."

"Negotiate?"

"Certainly. You've done that before. Make a deal so they won't sue you," Uncle Rudy said.

Mr. Smith looked hopefully at the wampetters.

Albert and Berthe nodded okay. And so commenced the Great Negotiation. For the rest of the day the adults sat around a table and talked, and argued and argued and argued. Encouraged by Uncle Rudy's suggestions, Albert and Berthe kept coming up with more things they wanted. They wanted all wampetters on the planet to have new travellers and for the Development Commission to give them all jobs and for wampetters to be in charge of anything that might affect galumpfs, trees, lakes or change the weather. Mr. Smith complained that he had to change the weather, it was awful, and he could only provide jobs for wampetters on other planets. He brought out charts and huge volumes of figures and maps and plans to show how much money had been spent and how much he needed to make.

The kids got restless. X and Y took Gartrude for a swim in the tank; Bill and Eloise went for a walk.

"I didn't know your parents were so greedy," Bill said.

"They're not," Eloise replied. "But they don't understand what's going on. They think it's like one of those bigscreen shows where if you keep asking for more then you'll get it. What does your Dad really want?" Eloise asked.

"To go somewhere else and start over. But he can't do that if you go to court."

"We just want things the way they were before," Eloise said.

Bill looked at Eloise and Eloise at Bill. They both knew what they had to do.

When they returned to the Smith's house the adults were screaming and worse. Mrs. Smith swung her purse at Berthe and Berthe tried to kick her back but Uncle Rudy jumped between them.

"We have a deal," Eloise announced.

The adults fell silent. Mrs. Smith lowered her purse. Berthe sat down.

Bill read from a piece of paper. "Dad, you agree not to do any more development on the planet, and not do any more advertising for tourists. In return, the wampetters agree to give back everything they have been given or bought on credit and agree not to go to court for anything the Commission did."

"That's right," Eloise said.

They both thought the adults would jump up and down and say Yes, Yes, Yes, but instead they grumbled and said No, No, No. Albert said they shouldn't have to give everything back and Mr. Smith said he needed more tourists to make more money. They resumed the argument.

The adults argued all night long. But when the sun crept above the horizon, Mr. Smith said: "I give up."

"Me too," said Albert.

Berthe and Mrs. Smith had already given up for they lay on the floor, snoring.

"We'll do what the kids said," Mr. Smith suggested.

"Sounds good to me," Albert said.

Within a few minutes Uncle Rudy had put everything down on paper in an official way and when everyone was awake, they all shook hands and stamped feet together, the human and wampetter ways of showing agreement.

Of course there was more work after this. The Tubs spoke at all kinds of meetings to convince wampetters that this was the best thing that could happen. Many wampetters did not like the agreement at first because they still wanted a new traveller. After hearing about how they could be sent to other planets, though, they said okay.

Mr. Smith spent an equal amount of time talking to his investors. They were angry because they wanted to become even richer than they were, but Mr. Smith explained that they would lose a great deal of money if the wampetters went to court. So the investors agreed as well.

On the first day of Winter the Tubs and Smiths gathered in the living room of the Smith's house to sign an Agreement to Stop Development. The invasion was over.

CHAPTER SEVEN

Wampetter of the Year

After signing the agreement the Smiths packed their house into five silvery suitcases and said good-bye. Bill tried to rub noses with Eloise but she was crying too hard.

"I'll write," Bill said.

"I'll write back," Eloise sobbed.

Then the Smiths took off in their ship for parts unknown.

"Well. No more tourists," said Berthe somewhat sadly.

"And no more adventures," said Gartrude gloomily.

"Thank goodness," said Albert. "We've had enough adventures for a whole lifetime. Now everything will get back to normal."

Normal was not what it was cracked up to be, though. Everyone missed something about the visitors. Berthe missed the bustle of the restaurant and the extra money she earned. Gartrude missed the tourists who laughed at her tricks and gave her big tips for directions, even if they were wrong. Albert missed the deluxe Super X Time-Shifter Lightning Model 7 traveller that had been theirs for a short time. Eloise missed Bill and Uncle Rudy.

It was the same all across the planet. Wampetters accustomed to new jobs and fancy stores where they could buy anything on credit, complained about their old jobs and dull wampetter stores. After a few months though, everyone settled back into old routines—with little changes that made a big difference.

The Tubs built themselves a new house where the old one had stood. The new house was larger and was packed with the modern conveniences they had come to enjoy in their city apartment.

Albert returned to his fishing column at the *Daily News of Yesterday,* but he also wrote stories about events on other planets. He said it was very important that wampetters understand what happens in the rest of the galaxy.

Berthe decided to become a ruler. She said, "We need some rulers who are wampetters. A ruler could have told us what that stupid Consent really meant."

Berthe took classes by bigscreen from one of the most prominent correspondence schools in their sector, the Loyola School of Rules and Exceptions. Every night Berthe told the rest of the family what she had learned, whether they wanted to hear it or not.

Gartrude went back to school, which she hated

until she learned arithmetic. She fell in love with numbers and took up celestial navigation. Every afternoon after school she calculated the best routes between various planets. She came up with a few shortcuts that soon were in general use. She also learned to read.

Eloise fell into a deep funk after the Smiths left. Nothing seemed to interest her and she was mad that no one paid any attention to what she had done. Every day she had to make her bed and do her homework and dry the dishes, just like any other kid and she had just saved the planet! It wasn't fair.

Eloise's spirits lifted when Albert mentioned the Wampetter of the Year award. Each year a special committee awarded a polka dot tie and a large sum of money to the wampetter who, "in the past year has done the most to promote the welfare of wampetters." The year before, the award had gone to the wampetter who invented shoes with built-in toenail clippers. This year it would go to someone who had done something much more impressive, Eloise decided. She wrote the awards committee a long letter about what she had done to save the planet—from her trip out to the Smiths' house, to rescuing Bill from Lake Wacawacawoo, to her dangerous, secret mission (she couldn't say too much about this for fear of getting in trouble) to her negotiation of the final Agreement.

The award ceremony was scheduled for halftime of the annual noseball championship game at Gus Galumpf Memorial Stadium. This year the defending champs, the Mudville Schnozzers, were to take on the

Pinocchio Rangers in the battle for the Proboscis Bowl.

The Tubs had just settled in their seats behind fifth base when Gartrude spotted a familiar figure stepping briskly up the aisle. "Look, it's Uncle Rudy." Uncle Rudy looked the same as ever, except now his hat was covered with plastic flowers.

"I was in the neighborhood and thought I'd stop by," Uncle Rudy said.

"Well come on, sit down," said Albert. "The game's about to start."

"There's little Jeen!" Gartrude shouted. The actor led a procession of wampetter dignitaries in purple and gold robes across the field. Gartrude called out to him but he did not notice.

The first half of the game was not especially exciting. The Pinocchios scored three runs, but did hardly any tricks and the Schnozzers couldn't seem to get their noses on the ball.

Then it was time for the award ceremony. The Mayor of Foom stepped up to the microphone in center field. "May I have the envelope please," he asked. An assistant handed the mayor a neatly folded piece of paper. The mayor held it up and then in one big motion ripped it in two. He examined the two halves.

"Whoops. Big mistake," he said. There was a short delay as the mayor and his assistant taped the paper back together. The mayor examined it carefully. He cleared his throat. "The winner is:" He paused and looked out at the crowd. He loved it when everyone listened to him, so he waited and waited, until everyone stamped their feet with impatience.

He cleared his throat again.

Eloise sat on the edge of her seat. Now everyone would know what she had done. She would be a hero. She would be a star.

"The winner is: little Jeen!"

The crowd exploded with applause. Eloise's jaw dropped. She could not believe it.

"For his selfless contributions to galactic entertainment, for promoting the good image of wampetters everywhere and in recognition of his new hit show, I hereby dub you Wampetter of the Year!"

Little Jeen stepped up to the podium and received the orange and green polka dot tie. "Thank you," he said. "And thank you all for watching my new show."

Little Jeen had just started a show called "Partners," in which he played a tough young wampetter detective who hunted down vicious intergalactic criminals with the help of a pretty human partner—played by none other than the beautiful Hannah. Hannah and little Jeen still hated each other, but after the old show was cancelled, neither were offered any other parts.

"I want you to know," little Jeen continued, "that Hannah would have come if she—" The crowd booed and whistled. Wampetters now hated Hannah as much as Hannah hated them. Little Jeen started over. "Hannah would have come, but she had to wash her hair." The crowd laughed and cheered.

"Seriously, though, you should know that I worked very hard to resolve the recent problems with the Development Commission. If I hadn't risked my life and my career, many of you would be toiling in the mines of Desarr, billions of miles from home." The crowd responded with thunderous acclamation.

"It's not fair!" Eloise cried. She jumped up and ran down the aisle toward the exit. Her feet moved just a little slower than the rest of her, though, and she tripped and fell head over heels down the stairs,

landing smack on her bottom. It was quite painful, but what was worse the whole crowd had seen it and was clapping. Wampetters love a good fall. Eloise dashed out to the parking lot, tears streaming down her face.

A few minutes later Uncle Rudy found her sitting on the ground, sobbing. He sat down beside her.

"I hate this planet!" Eloise said. "Hannah was right. Wampetters are stupid and mean. How can they give the award to little Jeen? He chickened out when it got scary. He's just a bratty kid who looks cute in pictures. It's not fair."

"No, it isn't," Uncle Rudy agreed.

"I want to go back with you. I don't want to live here any more."

"Your family would miss you terribly."

"Who cares. Mom and Dad are so stupid. They should have known what that Consent was about. They should have told me I'd never get the award. They just said, 'Let's hope for the best.'"

"Mmm," Uncle Rudy said.

"And what about you?" Eloise asked accusingly. "You knew what was happening with the Development Commission right from the beginning, didn't you?"

"Yes," he said.

"And you knew all the bad things they were going to do."

"Yes, I did."

"Then why didn't you stop it?" Eloise asked.

"Because that's not my job.You see, I'm an advisor. My job is to make suggestions."

"Suggestions?"

"That's right. When folks have a problem and are ready to listen, I give them hints about what they might do. But they have to solve the problem for themselves. If I had stopped your parents and all the others from signing the Consent, that wouldn't have solved anything. My brother, or someone else, would have tried again and it would have been even harder to fix."

"But we did all the work," Eloise observed.

"Absolutely."

"Okay, then. I have a problem. I should have gotten the award. Go up and tell them that. Make a suggestion," Eloise said.

"Are you sure?" Uncle Rudy asked.

"Yes," she said.

"Do you really want to be like little Jeen, or Hannah?" Uncle Rudy asked.

"No."

"Then I suggest you don't throw a tantrum every time you don't get what you want. Even if it's what you deserve."

Eloise glared at him. He had always been so nice and now he was acting mean like everyone else. She wasn't like little Jeen or Hannah. She really cared about other creatures, not just what they thought about her. But then, why did she care about the award so much? Saving the planet was much more important. She hung her head. "I guess I was just counting on it."

"I understand. We all want to be recognized for what we do." He paused. "I've got a little surprise for you."

Eloise looked hard at Uncle Rudy.

"Bill's birthday is next month," Uncle Rudy said. "And he's invited you to his party. I have here a round-trip first class ticket for you on the luxury liner Princess Mud if you'd like to come."

"Oh yes!"

"Now let's go back and see the rest of the game," Uncle Rudy said.

Later, Uncle Rudy came over to the Tubs' house for

a special meal. It began, as such meals always do, with a big dessert of pie and ice cream. Wampetters believe that since dessert is the best part of a meal, you should start with dessert so that if anything happens and you have to miss the rest of the meal, you don't miss dessert. Then, after all the regular courses are done, wampetters are ready for something sweet again, so they eat a second dessert: on this night it was cookies, fruit and cake. In the whole galaxy, no creatures eat the way wampetters do.

When the Tubs were completely stuffed, Uncle Rudy stood up to make an announcement.

"In all my years as an advisor," he said, "I have

never met a more courageous and dedicated family than you Tubs. Before coming here I consulted with the Grand Assembly of Advisors and we all agreed that you deserve some formal recognition of your efforts. We advisors don't generally believe in prizes and awards because they generally make folks forget what really counts, but we made an exception in your case. It is my privilege to give each of you a Noble Peace Prize."

The Tubs were speechless. Uncle Rudy took out a box and removed four small medals attached to ribbons. He hung a medal around each of their necks.

"To Albert Tub, for standing true to your word."

"To Berthe Tub, for determination and creative thinking."

"To Gartrude Tub, for saying what needed saying and doing what needed doing."

"To Eloise Tub, for courage and perseverance in defense of Planet Wampetter."

Then they all cried, for it was an occasion that cried out for crying.

In the early evening the Tubs walked in the hills and watched the stars come out. Uncle Rudy had already left. Apparently he was already late for a crisis in a nearby system.

Gartrude walked with Albert and chattered on and on about the stars. She identified each star in the sky and how far it was from Planet Wampetter: how many light years, how many sound years and how long it would take if you walked. "Saurus 10 is so far away that if you lived forever, from the beginning of time and spent your whole time walking from here to there, the universe would be dead by the time you got there. So it doesn't make much sense to walk."

"I agree," said Albert.

Eloise walked with her mother.

"Do you think we'll have visitors from other planets again?" Eloise asked.

"Certainly," Berthe said.

"Is that good?" Eloise asked.

"Certainly. We have a lot to learn about the rest of the galaxy."

"And they have a lot to learn about us," said Eloise.

"That's right," said Berthe.

"When I grow up I'm going to show everyone in the galaxy that wampetters are really smart."

Berthe smiled. "I think you've already done that dear."